EVERY

Ronnie Matthew

EVERY

Published by Pax, 2021

Cover design by Ken Dawson
www.ccovers.co.uk

ISBN 978-1-9168817-0-9

www.ronniematthew.com

EVERY

December 2nd _____

Dear Every,

I said your name as you were born. I shouted it over something the doctor said. I wanted it to be the first word you ever heard and although I'll never know, I believe that it was. It's my favourite word and now it's the name of my favourite person. You are only a few hours old, still warm from being so close to your mother's heart, closer than anyone has ever been. I hope one day you'll tell me what it's like being so near to it, or that you'll have a brother or sister so you can have conversations about it that are as private as the experience was. Listen to me, I say it like you'll remember. But I'd like to know, because God knows I've only ever been near enough to her heart to love it. Somehow that seems like a failing, perhaps on my part.

   You were in a womb not so long ago, and now you're next to me. I'm writing this facing you. You are on our bed. You are so small. It looks like there's an ocean around you and you're floating. And there hasn't been a storm for weeks. Your mother is sleeping, finally. She didn't want to for fear that she might not wake up, or that something would happen to you by the time she did, but I think that after nine months (nearly nine, you're a few days early) she had almost forgotten what it was like to sleep.

   And you, you haven't found out yet.

She almost looks more like a baby than you do. She's managed to curl herself up like one, and there you are, investigating the finer points of our ceiling out of what was not long ago, in the simplest moment I've ever been in, the newest pair of eyes in the world. I doubt the world knew what came into it. It couldn't have. And I hope it's still oblivious because that way you're only mine and your mother's. What nonsense, you can't even see the ceiling, can you? The doctors say you'll only see shapes amongst the black for a while yet. I wonder what that looks like.

I am not tired. I don't feel I have a right to be. Your mother just gave birth (obviously) and I imagine being born must be quite the event for you, that is if you've even noticed it's happened. So I decided to sit with you, and to watch you both, and write to you. To be honest I decided that a long time ago, the writing part at least. This is the beginning of your eighteenth birthday present. Every year on your birthday I'm going to write you a letter, and I'll give them all to you when you turn eighteen. Hopefully you won't be in the middle of hating me that day and end up burning them. But well, if you are (you will hate me at some point, of course you will, and in a way I'm looking forward to the experience), I suppose I can always give them to you on your twenty-first! I hope they give you an idea of what you are to your mother and I. To me, anyway. I can't speak for someone else, especially her, and a father can never speak for a mother. I'm only hours into this and I think I've learned that already. I am not a mother. It's something I'm just going to have to live with, perhaps in spite of. Maybe that's why I need letters.

When we asked our parent friends what to expect, they told us the world would change. Everyone seems to say that. It scares me to turn and look out of the window because you won't be in front of my eyes anymore, but I don't think it has changed. There are the same trees, the same rivers, same roads and absent god (don't you go getting that wrong) - there are even the same people. Mostly. I guess there have been a few changes at either end of the scale. You have a lot to learn about those things. About people. I'll warn you of that right now. Most of it you'll wish you could unlearn. Even when you're reading this, what you've learned by eighteen, I wish I could tell you it doesn't get much worse, but I can't. It's something we all have to figure out eventually. And when we do, something else confirms for us that we figured the wrong thing out too soon. The world can't have changed. It never does and it can't. But that's probably for the best. No one ever seems to get used to this world while they're in it, and if it went changing on us all the time I don't know how we'd cope. Maybe that's what's changed. I wish now that it would. For you. Even if it kills the rest of us.

You look too perfect to be human, far too much to be mine. I wonder how much of that perfection you'll have lost by the end of these letters. I wonder how much will have been taken from you by the end of this sentence.

I only hope you don't ever try to drain any from yourself, but I've never known anyone who has been able to resist. Whenever anyone tells you to avoid temptation, that's what they're talking about. I don't mean to talk to you like I expect you to fail in your life, but there's a reason children are precious and there's a reason it seems right that the old die. If it sounds like I expect something bad to happen, it's only because it's in your suffering that I believe I'll really meet you - but I'll die before I cause it. Then again, anything that does happen will have been brought on by your being alive, and for that your mother and I are wholly responsible. We have caused everything already. We are not sorry.

If it's in your suffering that I'll meet you, then it was in your mother's that I met her, and so she must not have suffered enough yet. Still a stranger and I know her better than anyone. The person she was before you came to her has gone away now, and I think it's best that she stays there. I won't tell you about her. Well, maybe one day. Just know that because of you she is better. I can see it in the way she sleeps. In her yawn I hear relief.

Sleep is coming for you now. You're fighting it away but soon you are to find out what a fortune it is.

(I looked up here, I didn't write for a minute, and I watched you fall into it.)

Your mother is waking, swapping places with you, and she's going to stop my thoughts running away until it's my turn to sleep. How they run when I dream, though.

Your mother just said Hello to me and she kissed you on the head. I'm going to join her on the bed, and we're going to watch you. Forever if forever lets us. I've said this ten times already in your tiny life, thought it a hundred and felt it once because the first time never ends, but I've not written it before, so: I love you, Every. I'm so glad you're here.

All my love,
Your father

(Oh my God I am a father!)

3/12/_____

Dad this is really nice. Sorry I found it and ruined the surprise. I was looking for something of Mum's because I missed her. It looks like you've got a lot of letters now. I won't tell you I found them so that way you can keep doing them. You sound really young it's funny. I love you too Dad and Mum as well.

Dear Every,

There's so much I remember of this first year with you that I don't think I have any room left for imagination. I don't need one or want one. I'm surprised I even have room for new memories, but you keep giving them to me and somehow they don't go away.

We do simple things. We don't do much. This is a quiet house for the most part, and one of the things I have enjoyed the most is watching you half awake in your chair, with your mother and I nearby. The odd word is spoken, but don't mind them. I like it when the window is open and there is a breeze. Your throat makes almost inaudible sounds, which I find funny. And sometimes I get a newspaper to read and peer over the top of, because that is what I've seen dads do on TV. Maybe I'll get a pipe.

I say it's quiet here, but then we have also found out this year that you like music. We have a piano. It's a little rickety, but it's your mother who plays it and she doesn't seem to mind. She makes up all these short, glassy phrases and I like the sounds because she made them. I can play a little guitar, and we have a few of them. Those are in tune, and when I play them for you it makes you shuffle around and wriggle, contorting your face like you're searching for an expression. Those sounds you make with your throat, who knows, maybe you're singing. In my mind you're singing.

You wouldn't believe how hard it's been not to write sooner - I wanted to write as soon as I put the pen down last year. But there is something in not writing that seems more loving than doing it, like I've let something stay where it came from, and that it never really needed to leave. Just know that there were things to write that weren't written. And that they were good, and beautiful, and that I hope you would have liked them. Somewhere there's a library without a wrong word in it. I'm smiling thinking about that. I guess I actually have written, just here and there. It was just notes to you, things I didn't want to forget, things I wanted you to find out. I've kept them somewhere - maybe I'll show them to you one day. Or you could show them to me - I'd put them in a box for you and you could look through them when I'm old. When I'm fading. When I'm remembering. When I'm confusing the two.

I could watch you.

So I do still have room for an imagination! That's so interesting to me now. Can you remember imagining something? I mean if you stop imagining it but remember that you did. Does it just become a memory? What's the difference? Answer me that, when I'm old. It would make so much real, like the way you were here so long before you were born. Imagined, and so real. Don't worry, you don't have to live up to our imaginings of you. You've already beaten them out of us. Just by being here you've shown us our thoughts couldn't even come close to what you are. Maybe we'll catch up. Maybe you'll get away completely. I'd prefer neither, I think. But, well, you'll always run away. Of course you will.

We have a recording of your heart, you see, and we listen to it sometimes. I have it on now. The doctor let us make it in the hospital, and we play it back on the computer and we loop it so it doesn't stop. It's just a few beats from your earliest moments but it sounds like you're going to live forever, or that forever is going to live in you. With us. We fall asleep to it often.

Those are peaceful nights, ones where your whimpers sound like song. Your heart will always run away from where that recording keeps us. I don't think we care.

Most of the presents today were for us. You did get some toys to cuddle (not that you have, not that you will) and a book with very large writing and even bigger pictures. Those came from our friends. You have no aunts or uncles, and for maybe the first time my growing up without a brother or sister seems like I missed out on something. I'll try to make that different for you. There are no grandparents. Your mother's father is the only one still alive, but not to her, and she not to him. It's a shame but we don't talk about it. If you ever meet him, lie to him and pass on our love. If he gets it from a lie at least he'll get it from somewhere.

I never knew my dad. He died when I was small. An infant. I don't remember him but I remember a deep voice which my mind appears to attribute to him. It's not like mine. Depending on which version of the story I got, he either died of a heart attack, in a road accident, from some inherited disease, or sometimes he just went in his sleep. I don't suppose it matters much. He's dead and that's that. It wilted my mother. Maybe that's why her story shifted as much as it did. I learned pretty young to stop trying to talk about it.

How she would have loved to meet you. It was the aftermath of a heart attack that got her, though the stubborn old thing stuck around for a few days. Your mother was pregnant with you and the bump had just started to show. She used to let your grandmother put her hand on her stomach, and sometimes I think mum even forgot I was there. She died knowing you were on the way, like seeing you coming was enough of a solace. I guess that means I was never the solace. I'm a little bitter about that, if I'm honest.

Two of our friends (they have a baby on the way now as well) bought us a picture frame. We're supposed to put you in it but we won't. You'll know this now, and you'll have noticed before you knew, but we don't take pictures of you. Or of each other. Or of places we've been or of people we've loved. All those moments go. All a photograph ever shows is that right before it was taken, something was precious to someone. And that when it was taken, it was gone. We don't have to lose any of it. The smiles on your mother's face today were slighter than the ones a picture can keep. I don't catch them on her that often, but I have seen them coming. There was a kind of smile the day you were born that I don't think she could ever smile again. Warped. Relieved. It's the kind that only happens once, like the ones I've seen people show on deathbeds. They just come out of you.

Her smiles seem to have seen the peace I've wished upon her. Of course, that peace is you. You are mine too. But it is her smile you've changed. It's taken a year but now I can see that it's settling in. I can't wait for you to be old enough to know what's in it, I really can't. And I can't wait to see what's in yours. I haven't seen one yet but I'm waiting. The camera's ready to be turned away!

Don't though. Don't get old enough. Don't get any older. Stay there, stay asleep, and let it be your first birthday forever. Never say a sentence - a word was enough. And never let me know what your first thought was because the word implies so much. Stay here.

Stay here.

Love,
Dad

3/12/_____

What do you mean that's my heart? I don't understand.

I have a picture of her. I should show it to you.

Dear Every,

Every time you walk you walk away from me. I'm sure
that's not true, but it may as well be when I look. You just
turn away. But we watch you. Your mother holds my
hand then gives me a look that says it's nothing, and then
she gives my hand a squeeze that says she didn't want to
say out loud that it's not. With her next to me you never
go too far away, and I don't blame you. She's a very good
reason to come back. She believes the same of you, and
she is right. I get scared when I'm the only one with you,
like alone I'm not enough to come back to, and the thing
I imagine most is the first step you took with neither of
us watching you. What did you come back for, Every?
Her, probably.

The last time we watched you walk away, you fell in
the rain. It was nothing painful and you didn't bleed, but
your mother did what she always does and rushed over to
you like the world was ending three feet in front of you,
and you were about to crawl into it.

It is my nightmare that you keep on crawling, and that
oblivion's reflection is in your eyes. I'd say it's the same
dream every night but it's every moment. I never knew
there was a spectrum of blacks until I dreamed that your
eyes contained every shade. When I look at you awake
they are so blue that I don't think an entire sky could even
be a drop in them, but in the nightmare they are so black

and I've never seen anything that black. Now I know what a nightmare is: us preparing ourselves for something beyond us that we have to see sooner or later. I'm scaring myself now. I hope I'm not scaring you. This doesn't make any sense and I know that but I can't bring myself to cross it out. Ignore it.

I'm doing it again, aren't I? Talking about you like there's no hope for you. Please understand that I'm just scared, and I hope that by the point in your life that you're reading this you'll have proven all my fears to be wastes of emotion. Laugh at me. I hope to God that you're laughing at me.

You see, when you fell and your mother ran over to you, you were up before she made it. Then for a few seconds after you stood, she was knelt before you. She didn't hang her head out of piety to you (something I would have been guilty of) - she just looked up at you like your face was the only star in the only night. She opened her eyes wide underneath you, waiting for you to cry as though she could catch your tears. And she would fill her eyes - her head, her heart, her lungs - with your tears if she could, but you rarely cry. Nothing ever seems to make you sad. It scares us both.

I heard your mother wince as she got up, and she told me later that it was her stomach.

I know what's going to happen to her.

~~Love~~,

I thought I was done. I thought I was done and then I kept thinking of what I just said. I think I want to tell you about when your mother went to Michigan. It's a funny thing, telling a story second hand. She went there before I knew her, and I know what she has told me and she's told me several times, but of course with the way a mind works, I could be wrong about any of it.

It was in an October. I don't know which one, but it was several ago and she was young, maybe seventeen or so, a little while before I met her. She had been arguing with her father, and by arguing I mean he had screamed at her for days and she had taken it. The alcohol on his breath turned the air pungent until he inhaled it back. I don't know what the problem was, and from everything I have heard about him I imagine neither did he. The arguing had weathered her. He would keep the screaming and the swearing going and so too the accusation that it was all your mother's fault and her mother's as well although what the 'it' was was lost to them all. A closed door between them was no barrier but your mother put it there anyway. It may as well have been paper. The routine of it was that the stereo started after the door was closed, and she would wait it out over a couple of hours with the remnants of the argument still teasing her from the hallway. But that day the volume kept notching up, and the same Beatles song kept looping back round. I can't remember its name but even now if it comes on in a coffee shop, she ups and leaves and lets the coffee go cold. He had lit cigarettes and left them in an ashtray outside her room so the smoke funnelled in and got right in her nose. She waited until she heard him stumbling around downstairs to make a run for it out of the house with a backpack and some money. She made it out of the front door onto the street and she heard him coming after her, screeching at her to get back inside. He called out to her, 'Swine!' and she didn't answer. Then he rasped something embittered like, 'Yeah, just walk out then,' and she did. I don't know where her mother was in all of this. I think sometimes she was as drunk as he was. Your mother heard the stereo from all the way at the bottom of the street and a way around the corner. She couldn't hear him cursing her from there but she knew he probably was.

She took a train to the airport and a couple of hours later she was between countries. Whenever she told me this she was always surprised that they just let her get on a plane and go but I told her they'll let you do anything if it's legal and you have the money, and sometimes you only need the money.

The trip was about six hours long and halfway pleasant for someone who just walked out of a shitty man's shitty house. Food on a plastic tray and all the sparkling water she wanted. It was a fairly empty flight and they let her put the armrests down and her feet up. Her mind circled on the thought of how little she would care if the plane's engine busted and they fell out of the sky. She closed her eyes and imagined it. She opened them and tried to stop.

She imagined herself falling still strapped into the seat, the tremendous noise and the absence of fear. She felt sad for the stewardess, who she thought would be frightened, and sad to die. Your mother has since told me that it's when you're trying *not* to think about dying that you should probably start worrying about it. Well, no one died. Not that time.

She got to the city late at night and called the cheapest places to stay that she could find. She paid for two weeks at a hostel that had plywood walls between the beds and chicken wire across the top. I guess that seemed like a good deal but when two weeks' rent costs about the same as one night at a chain hotel, something's not going to be great. The only word she remembered the man behind the desk saying was 'cash,' and something about no refunds.

There were people smoking inside and it choked her like home did so she went to bed with the sheet across her face. She was awake all night as she'd slept on the plane and the morning seemed like it cheated her in staying away so long. The night was loud. There was fighting and cackling and someone even yelled at the microwave because it didn't ping when it was done. There was knocking. She wasn't sure if it was on her door or the one next to it, but the doors had padlocks on them and her eyes were shut and there was no way any of those things were opening.

She waited until morning for the bathroom. She walked up the windowless corridor to the end and around a corner and past someone playing a guitar. She didn't recognise the music but it made her think at least not everything there was awful. The guitarist didn't see her and just kept playing, which she liked. A sign pointed upstairs to the bathroom. It was a shared one with a door that wouldn't close. There were four toilet cubicles inside and a shared shower that only had a curtain, one of those blue plastic ones that sticks to you while you're in there. The walls were tiled but moulded and moulded bad. The floor was too. She noticed that her teeth were clenched. She heard the shower stop running and a woman came out not a lot cleaner than someone unwashed, and then the woman wrapped a rotted towel around some of herself and left. Your mother looked at the shower. The plughole had thick mould around it and the water trickled through an open slit. Someone had toenailed it in. She figured she'd wait.

In one of the cubicles a toilet failed to flush. A woman came out and said, 'Sorry girl, I think it's busted. Fucking place is a mess.'

She decided to wait for that too.

The walk into the city itself was about twenty minutes across a bridge that had a burgundy fence at the side and a nice view through it if she put her eyes close enough. It was a clear day and the water was still. The noise of the cars clattered in the metalwork and there were trains above her and they shook it too. She looked out again and the city streetlights were just turning off as the lifts started going up. She tried to work out how high up she was and if dying would be a sure thing if she fell. She thought it probably would be, if it wasn't for the fence. She kept moving in case any of the morning runners thought that was what she was thinking. The bridge rattled under her as they passed and she could feel it in her shins.

There was a ramp down to the pavement when she got to the other side of the bridge. The wind was light but still enough to drag the streetlitter across the pavements and the road. She thought the allure the city had from a distance seemed a sham. A clock above a coffee shop sign told her it was about seven twenty. She worked out she was in the south of the city and she figured that if she walked north she'd have to find a toilet somewhere. When she did it was in a small park. It was the kind of toilet where the door only covers part of you. She was quick.

The more she walked, the more the city grew into the day and the more the city ignored her. Most of the people had spilled out from underground trains on their way to work. There were others out walking dogs and others still were out with no one and nowhere else to be. She came across a group of people standing around outside a library. If she stood with them, she thought, she might look like she wasn't lost. They went in when the library opened and she followed them. Almost all of them headed straight up a ramp towards the computers. She approached one on the edge of a row but the screen said something about account numbers. She kept moving to make it look like she knew where she was going. She looped back to the ramp and past the counter. The person at the counter said something to her in a thick accent that she couldn't quite understand, and when she looked at him and opened her mouth to speak, it felt like her tongue was about twice as wide as it should be.

'Books,' he said. 'Did you get any books?' His voice was a little clearer that time.

'No.'

'Nothing?'

'Do you want to check?' She held up her bag and the man looked at her.

'No, miss.'

She left.

She thought about the computer. She had left home in such a hurry that she had forgotten to set her phone for travelling. She had not told her mother where she was and she regretted it. Her throat tightened. She looked around on the street where the library spat her out. There were breakfast places and office blocks and houses that had been turned into flats. There was nothing around her that said anything about computers. A ticker sign on the other side of the street went back and forth between red and green. The red one said DRUGS and the green one said PHARMACY. She'd heard all about those American pharmacies. She crossed the street and went in. She walked the aisles and found the painkillers. She didn't recognise any of the names so she picked a couple of bottles out. At the counter the man told her one of them was on offer, so he picked another bottle out for her. She thanked him. She put the bottles in her bag and walked to the park. She found a bench in a quiet spot and opened one of the bottles. She unscrewed her water with a fist of pills in her hand, and she started taking them a few at a time. It was neither the first nor the last time she had done it, but she insists she's never done it to try to die. I don't get that.

She watched the ducks and the dogs. The stomach pains started about an hour after. She crossed her legs and leaned back into the bench and looked at the water and listened to the chatter. She thought it would be a nicer morning with a coffee in her hand so she got one and then went back to the bench. She thought about how far away she was from burning a hole into her gut. Pretty far, it turned out. It had cleared up by lunch.

It was quite a hunt finding somewhere to send a message home. It wasn't really something people had to do anymore. See, Every - we're not that old. The place she ended up finding was in a busy part of town. It was an internet cafe and it was probably there for tourists. She paid for a tea and paid an extra dollar for the computer password.

'It's username for the username and it's password for the password,' the lady at the counter said.

Your mother stood there and looked down. She had taken the words in but that seemed all she could do with them. Even repeating them to herself was a task blocked off by some strange obstacle. She thought walking away was better than standing still so she took her tea to the table and looked at the screen. The sounds from everyone else's keyboards sounded like they were coming from her own bones. The computer wanted the username and password.

She went back to the desk. 'Sorry,' she said. 'What was the login?'

'It's username for the username and it's password for the password.'

'Okay.'

She sent her mother a message about coming home.

The stomach pains came back on the plane.

Maybe that's not a story you needed to know. The way your mother tells it, it's funnier. The way I hear it, it's not very funny at all.

3/12/_____

She never told me that.

Dear Every,

This year your body has gone from perfect to scarred. It's the strangest thing to see. Touch just under your chin. (I'm touching it now - you think I'm tickling you and you're laughing). I wonder how common that is. That a parent touches their child and it feels like something other than fear. It really never should. I'd say it's a strange thought, but I don't think it is. You just told me to stop (I actually did start tickling you) and you called me Daddy, and even I smiled, and even I laughed. I'm smiling through my own fear - thank you. This is one of those moments it's worth forgetting the rest of the world for. I hope you've had one of those moments - from me, from your mother, from anyone.

I don't ever smile through your fear because I don't think there is any. None that I've seen. I think that's where some of my own comes from, wondering why it is you're never scared. If your finger is still on your chin, that's where you bled from. The scar is so well in line with the curve of your chin that it's almost like God is even injuring you perfectly. There's no way around that damned kind of perfection. I'm sure you'll know by now how you got it, but as yet I've never told you. I will do so now.

There's a grate in front of the fireplace. I don't know if it's there anymore of if the fireplace is - whoever owned the house before us blocked the chimney so it's just a decoration these days - but if it is then so is a speck of your blood. You fell onto it. You're always falling so I don't know why we even had it there. It's our fault really. Falling is the one thing so far that I've noticed you get from me. I'm always on the lookout for something else, but there is nothing in your face from anyone but your mother. You've laughed at me falling so many times! Whoops! I'm glad I can get that emotion out of you so easily. It's important. I suppose you were running around. Your mother and I were in the other room and we heard you fall. It's an unmistakable sound, like a cowpat landing in a puddle, and we laughed like we always do. Your mother's face looked like a beaten wrinkle stretching back out to beauty. It was such a thing to see. You must have been clambering back up while we were shaking off the laughter. 'She's funny,' your mother said. I nodded, still grinning, eyes on the chequered kitchen floor linoleum. I did that slow chuckle you do when you're stopping yourself from laughing, and your mother said, 'Shit.' I remember thinking she pronounced the T a lot more than she usually did when she swore. When I looked up she was already rushing off to the doorway, and my head had jerked up so quickly that the floor pattern was still flickering in my vision. I saw the blood through it. I had no idea how much blood could come from the chin of a child. 'Jesus, Every.' Your mother's voice cracked. She made it over to you and cupped your chin and tilted your head back. 'I thought it was her throat,' she said. Your throat was covered in blood. But there was an ebb at your chin that, compared to that at least, was a relief. 'Fuck,' your mother said quietly, nearly privately. 'Fuck.' She shook her hair back a couple of times. There was blood in her fringe. It was the weirdest thing to see, you just stood there letting your mother touch your face while blood fell out of you. Your mother's breathing was heavy, and in the gaps between the dumping out of breath, yours just whispered along. There wasn't a tear in your eye or for a mile behind it. If anything you looked, well, a little sleepy. That moment I had with you just now, well this was the opposite. This was the kind of moment you wish was accompanied by something else, anything else, because even the snap of my own toe would at least be a distraction from it. Never have one of those moments, Every. Avoid them the best you can.

When your mother calmed down, she let go of your chin for a moment to see if it was still bleeding. There was this odd look between you and her when you seemed to become just as calm as each other, reflections of each other. It wasn't something I liked seeing. She put her thumb back over your cut and there was a trail of blood leaking down her arm to where her own cuts used to seep through her sleeve. 'It's okay,' she said. She looked at the blood on her arm. 'It's okay.' I stepped away.

It wasn't long after I met her that I first saw her bleed. It was through clothing and across a day. She was wearing a thin, off white top and we were at that stage of our relationship where we talked about everything because everything was new to us. I looked at her eyes, and I watched her mouth the way I tend to when people talk to me, but as the conversations went on, the more these tiny patches of blood worked through her sleeves. She gripped at her cuffs with two fingers and turned her arm in, but after a while she would forget, and a while after that the blood would seep through some more. Well she told me later that she never did forget but that hiding it all the time made her tired.

You're scarred now. It was always going to happen. If there's an upside to it, it's that it looks kind of pretty now, just a little white thing smiling when you lift your chin. I wish you weren't scarred this early on, and I hope nothing else happens for a while, but I must admit in part to admiring it. Maybe it's how brave you were that I admire, but then maybe it just didn't hurt. I suppose that's possible. But surely it was scary? Wasn't it? It must have been. You've looked at it in the mirror and asked me what it is, so maybe you don't remember, but you might just be appeasing me. I told you that you fell. The same has undoubtedly happened with your mother, and she probably tells you a lot more. She's a lot more on the nose than I am about things like that. I imagine she traces the trail of blood from your chin, to your throat, to her hand and down her arm. And I imagine she traces her arm with your finger. And I bet you stare into that mirror together and share your faces and your wounds and that moment and everything else I can't share with either of you that I wish so much that I could. All I can do is watch. I'm glad there's a place where you can share it, but I'll be damned if I wouldn't like to see that mirror in pieces one day. But there would be so many reflections, and we'd all get lost in them. I wish it could just be a cut, then a scar, then a forgotten thing, and I wish everything could be a forgotten thing including me half the time, and I just don't understand things the way they are, and I don't understand people like you and your mother, and I wish I didn't think you were so much the same, but I fear so badly that you are, or that you will be. I must seem so simple to you. I don't share in any of this.

You still think I'm tickling you when I touch your chin. I've never told you this story properly but I've written it down now so in a way I have, and it's nice that I can just keep it here, with me, until it's something we can finally share, like our laughter just a few minutes ago, because it's gone now.

Love,
Dad

3/12/_____

I don't remember cutting my chin. I touched it when you told me to though. I hope you don't touch it for a while because it's weird now. You've told me you like it before. Sorry I got Mum's arm messy. I know what happened to her arms. It's really obvious. I won't let you know you've told me any of this. Don't worry.

December 2nd _____

Dear Every,

I'd like to tell you some of the things your mother and I talk about. It strikes me that we never really talk when we're around you. I mean, of course we talk around you, but for some reason none of our serious conversations happen when we are. I suppose we're trying to keep that kind of thing away from you, but that's laughable really, isn't it? You wouldn't understand or remember. What a lucky way that is to be! We usually talk when you're asleep, when your door is open just a crack to let a little light in, and downstairs we talk quietly so our voices don't go in with it. You haven't got used to a closed door yet. We've tried closing it before and you don't scream like I imagine other children do, you just get out of bed and open it again and we don't notice it until we go to bed as well. We leave it. You're so silent.

I do wonder if you know more of what we talk about than we think. I'm sure you'll have been in bed awake and heard something through the door - this isn't a big house. I hope we're still in the same one now, by the way, that's always been something I've wanted for you. The comfort of knowing that your room is where you grew up, that the table is where you've eaten a thousand dinners, and that those marks on the door are from where we've marked how much you've grown. I want you to be able to come home long after we're both gone, when you're nearly gone yourself, so you can see yourself inching back towards the height you were all those years ago, however many that may be. That would be an interesting space to be in, to fill the exact same space you did before your life really happened to you. You see, if you can make memories like those there will be no need for a single photograph of anything. And if we live somewhere else now, and when someday you leave, and if you never form those memories in the first place, then well, you know where they would have been. This house has a lot for you, and so do I.

I was saying that maybe you know more than we think. Perhaps you've heard us talk about our health, about our money, or about things that have happened to us that linger a little too closely. I have a proclivity towards worry. I know that. And so I will work away from that for you, and refrain from relaying those woeful conversations, and I'll start you off with something happy. The day I first told your mother about you.

I knew your name before I knew hers. She wasn't 'your mother' yet, she was just Eleanor, somebody I finally got to spend a whole weekend with, but I think I knew even then who she was bound to be. This would have been about ten years ago now, I suppose. Gosh, that went fast. It was summer, and a lovely day, and while we were laying in the park she asked me to read her something I'd been writing. I did a lot of writing back then. These letters are about all I do of it now because I feel like there's very little else worth imagining with you finally in my life, but I think

I was actually quite good at it, although I am embarrassed to say so. I don't have anything to show you, I'm afraid, because I made a point of never keeping anything I wrote for very long, whether it was a letter or a novel (lots of the former, only one of the latter - and only your mother ever saw it) because I quite simply liked the idea of writing something and just leaving it there. That way it just exists for what it is, as we all should. Now I rather wish I had something for you, maybe a children's story I could read to you at bedtime, but I don't have anything. I don't even remember if I ever wrote one.

I think your mother might have kept a poem or two (I gave her my copies because although I didn't like them, she wanted to see them) but I won't ask for them back. You can ask her about them one day, if you want. But they're hers really, as these letters are yours. I like that idea, of writing something for someone and just, as I said before, leaving it with them. Part of your imagination that's just for them.

She knew I'd been writing something. She asked me to bring it with me, though I really wasn't sure if I'd let her see it. It was written as a letter, as the beginning of an eighteenth birthday present, from a father to his daughter, who he had named Every, a name he had chosen long before she was born. It isn't the letter at the start of this, don't worry, but it was something I wanted to do and I couldn't bring myself to wait until you actually came, so I did it as a story instead. It did seem a bit dangerous, possibly precarious, but it never went beyond that first letter, which I no longer have. She wanted me to read it to her right there in the park, and I explained why I was uncomfortable with that, and the fact that you were already in some ways real to me, but she just smiled at me more and more - brightly, openly - so I read it. I could not help it. I left it there, with her, and I think she appreciated it. Well, clearly she did, because she married me! As I read it aloud I had half an eye on the words and the other eye and a half on her. She had hers on me, completely, and as I read, 'Love, Dad,' she let out a whimper, a murmur, some sound of approval, or of acceptance.

There are moments, and you'll know this if you write yourself, when someone can fall in love with something you've made, and they mistake it for falling in love with you, and so do you, and it's an odd feeling, because you can never really know if that's what's happened or not. I guess it's not that way with your mother and I, but it's something I was wary of. Maybe it's why I never kept my writing. Don't ever make anything beautiful, Every. People mistake it for you.

We spent a lot of time in parks now that I think of it. There was another day, in a park in London, where we finally spoke about you as someone we might become the parents of. It's strange to think of that conversation now, and it was strange to have. It was the first time she had spoken about you by name. 'It'd be nice to bring Every here, don't you think?' she asked.

We were walking under a long row of trees. There was a playground and an ice cream hut off to our left. We heard the children playing. 'Yeah, I think she'd like it. Lots to do.'

'What kinds of things would you do with her?' She still had on that enormous smile, and I noticed for the first time that her teeth were kind of small.

'I don't know,' I said. 'Depends what she'd like. Maybe I'd take her on the pedal boats. Everyone likes those.'

'I like those,' she said. 'And there's room for three.'

She looked down a little, holding her hands in. The edges of her smile receded. 'You know,' she said, and then she stopped. 'If we're really talking about this.' She stopped again. 'What if Every was a boy?'

It's not like the thought hadn't crossed my mind. I could dream of you all day long - playing with you, joking with you, being slightly sarcastic to confuse you a little - and the knowledge that there's no guarantee you'd even be a girl lingered like a sore knuckle. But I had also worked out how to answer the question. 'It'd be fine,' I said. We stopped walking. I think she stopped first. 'We'd just call him something else. We'd think of something nice.' Your mother's smile didn't return, but it didn't fade any further either.

I'll be honest though. I was relieved you were a girl. I'm sure I'd have loved you just as well if you were a boy, but I can't say I don't have any doubt about that. I'm not proud of that feeling. I am stuck with it, however.

I held my face as straight as I could. I was very aware of how tightened my chin felt. My gaze turned to a stare and your mother's face broke into a blur. There was green behind her, the occasional tint of brown. She put her hand on mine. 'Hey,' she said. 'You okay?'

'Yeah. Just thinking.' The colours separated back into shapes and your mother's face took centre stage again.

'I never told you,' I started. 'I always thought Eleanor would be a nice middle name. Every Eleanor.'

She gargled some kind of sound from her throat. I think she was trying to laugh. It didn't work.

'I always liked it. Even before I knew you.'

'Hmm. I don't know.' She inhaled through her nose and opened her mouth before she spoke again. 'I think that would be a problem.' Same breath, all of it.

'Ah.'

'I'm sorry. That feels weird. That's all.'

'It's fine. I can choose something else. Or you could.'

'Maybe. If that's happening.'

Sometimes our conversations broke off so quickly it's like I didn't know where they had gone. Next thing I knew we were walking through the gardens and I was finding out how much your mother knows about plants. Seriously, ask her anything.

Well, in the end she did choose your middle name. She chose Hope, even though Every Hope sounds a bit corny, because essentially that's what you are. To me and to her. And thanks for coming, as she would perhaps put it. She always puts things so simply for me. So I can understand. Every, you've changed more than I knew existed.

So did your mother. Right now I'm looking at you, you're just colouring something in, a picture of a lion by the looks of it, and I know that you are here by the grace of the woman I got to spend warm days with in those parks. So in a way it's perfectly right that I see so much of her in you, because that's where she is. It's funny thinking of that conversation about having you - bear in mind we'd made no commitment to each other, it really came from nowhere - I can barely believe I've had that conversation with someone. Even looking at you, I can't believe it. The past, everything that was so magical about it, seems like a wind now, one that blew away a long time ago and all that's left is its chill on my face. I wish the same thing happened to bad memories, but for some reason those always seem real, and present. I really ought to go through the past a bit more, one day. And wow, I wonder what's in yours?

Until you were born, your mother gave me the most perfect moments of my life in that park in London. I kind of want to go back and get them. But that 'perfect moment of my life' phrase is one I've stolen from your mother, because apparently, and this is something else it's hard for me to believe, I gave her the most perfect moment of hers, after a house party we once went to. She doesn't have the best of pasts, and I wish I'd been in more of it to ease it for her. I've told her before that had I been there I would have made it all go away, but really I don't know if I'm the right kind of person to save someone. I can't promise anything like that. Thinking about it, and I don't tell her this, I'd probably just have run away and regretfully left her to it. She used to worry a lot about the extent to which her past would be a problem in our present. She still does. I remember the night of the party. We had been at a friend's house for their birthday. There weren't many people there, and we did know a few of them, but on the way your mother told me she couldn't stop digging her fingernails into her palms. We stopped near the doorstep. 'Are you okay?' I asked.

'Yes,' she said. She always said Yes instead of Yeah when she was lying. She held her jaw so far up and back that she probably could have chewed on her own teeth. 'Come on,' she said, and she walked towards the door. Her hand slipped out of mine. Well, I think she might have pulled it.

She knocked on the door and someone we didn't know answered. 'Hey,' they said.

I said, 'Hi,' and your mother smiled with her lips closed and her eyebrows up.

We went in and found Christopher in the kitchen. It was his wife Mia's birthday. We'd missed most of the food but there were still some nibbles left and we helped ourselves to cheese. I think there were more kinds there than I'd even heard of. Christopher saw us and came over. He handed us each a beer. 'I didn't think you guys were going to make it,' he said. He'd dressed up a bit. He had a suit jacket on without a tie.

'We were just a little late leaving,' I said.

'It's been good,' he said. 'Pretty chilled.'

'Is Mia around?' your mother asked.

'She's upstairs. In the spare room I think.'

'I'm going to go and say Happy Birthday.' She couldn't get out of there quickly enough.

Christopher and I carried on talking for a while and he told me about a car they were buying and a town they wanted to move to. He was always going on about things like that. I don't remember which town it was that time. I told him we were staying put.

'How's Elle doing these days?' He was the only person who called your mother Elle. 'We don't see much of you guys.'

Well, them and everyone else. We'd met Christopher and Mia on a walking weekend when we were dabbling in friendships one summer, and your mother always got along with Mia fairly well so we'd stayed in touch.

'She's not too bad. Thanks.'

He looked me hard in the eyes like he wanted my answer to follow itself up. I waited it out.

'Good,' he said. 'That's good.'

He kept that gaze on me, smiling to invite me to speak, and there was an encouraging nod, like the ones journalists use when they interview famous people. His grin subsided after ten seconds or so and he let out a deflated breath. 'Well, I'm going to mingle. Have a good night. Beer's over there.' He walked off towards a group of three men, and when he got there he slapped one of them on the back. From there I thought I knew the guy, but when he turned round to greet Christopher, I had no idea who it was.

If I'm going to have to be at a party the last thing I need is a conversation. All that people watching is hard enough to keep up with. I leant against a table and sipped my beer. Next thing I knew I was on my third one but I put it down before it was finished. I drink a little here and there but I've never much liked the jellylegs. I must have been sipping drinks for an hour or so by the time I thought to go and check on how your mother was. I heard her and Mia giggling on my way up the stairs, and the door to the spare room was open so I let myself in.

'There you are,' Mia said. She was sat on the floor, leaning against the bed. Your mother was by the wall with her knees up in her chest. It smelled a little of smoke in there but I couldn't see any cigarettes.

'Hi,' I said. I turned to your mother. 'You okay?'

'Yes.' There were empty bottles beside her. She had one heck of a glassy look in her eyes and her gaze wandered when she tried to look at me. 'You want to see what we can do?'

I stared at the both of them.

'You ready?' your mother asked. She spoke across me, like I wasn't there. Mia nodded and straightened up. Her hair dangled dead straight. She started singing a tune that I didn't recognise with words about a couple of bandits. It was playing quietly through the stereo. I looked up the words afterwards and it's by a man named Townes. You should look him up. It's a pretty song. Your mother and Mia sang it together, and then Mia started keeping a beat by hitting the floor. Your mother joined in and they managed to syncopate some percussion to it. The thing is, they were hitting the floor *hard*, fists driving straight onto the wood and their knuckles catching on splinters. I wondered why I hadn't heard them from downstairs. Mia's voice dropped out first and your mother's lingered a little while longer. She sang only to herself, and her voice lasted longer than it usually did. And then it faded out too and it was only the punching left. Mia's arm slowed and her fingers looked sore. She peeked at her skin while your mother carried on. 'See,' your mother said. 'This is fun.'

She hit the floor with her right hand, and she hit it right beside her knee. She lost the rhythm and the song may as well have been noise. The wake of each blow just about touched the soles of my shoes. I tried to step away, but it was only a shuffle, and it didn't work.

'Eleanor, stop,' said Mia. She cradled her hands together beside her lap.

'It's okay. I can't even feel it. See.'

She kept going.

'Eleanor.' Mia's voice had lowered. She slid over and put her hand where your mother's fist was landing. 'Stop it,' she said. Mia looked straight at her and winced when a fist landed on the back of her hand. That was the last punch. Your mother had worn her knuckles down and she sat there scraping off the skin against the floor. All of those flecks you get if you take a fall on tarmac.

Mia turned to me. Her head and shoulders fell in a little. 'Well?' Her voice rose as she said it. She hit a high enough pitch to give my neck a real jolt.

'I'll take her home,' I said.

'I don't want to go home.'

'You should go home, honey,' Mia said. 'Get some sleep.'

'What were you doing that for?' I asked.

'It was just some fun. Obviously it got out of hand.'

'Obviously.'

'Well, who stopped her?' Mia asked, but I didn't really get the impression she had meant it as a question. Your mother hit the floor again.

We left, and on the way out your mother scraped her hand along the walls. Playfully, she thought. I followed her. She left invisible flecks of flesh beside me. I was a fleck of flesh beside her. Mia saw us out.

I don't know what happened to Mia and Christopher. I know they moved away like Christopher said they would, but they didn't stay in touch.

It was a short walk home, maybe five minutes if you're not taking your time too much. They lived just down the road from the school. It was a quiet walk home. We were two pieces of litter drifting in the breeze. I was the bigger piece.

I was just ahead of your mother as we turned off the main road and onto our street. I felt the drop in the air as she stopped walking. I turned to her. She was squeezing her hurt hand. Either she was nursing the feeling back in or she was trying to squeeze it out. The moon was low enough to be mostly hidden behind houses and trees, but what light there was draped itself at your mother's back. It wasn't at its brightest, but it was better than nothing. The streetlights here are shit.

She spoke with a burst of breath at the start and a tired exhalation at the end. 'Is there too much worrying stuff about me?'

I took her hand, the hurt one. It wasn't bleeding but the bruises were coming up big. There were tears in her eyes, and goodness knows what behind them. I said, 'No. I love you.'

She looked up at me. Christ, she was tired. My mind chased back through the evening, knowing then that it was something it had to remember. All the cadences and inflections, all the faces and their wearings. Some of them already lost.

It wasn't the first time I had said that I loved her, and we had gone through the routine enough times that I didn't need her to answer it. I took her other hand too. She leant into me and let out a flurry of shaking breaths and a thimble's worth of tears.

This is cheesy as all hell, but your mother told me later that that was the moment when everything that had ever happened to her seemed finally to be okay. She said that nothing could haunt her anymore, at least not without some kind of a fight. She said that for that moment, the pain in her hand stepped aside for a second, and she believed that peace was a state she could attain, because she felt it, just momentarily, then.

Apparently I did that for her in that one moment. She does it for me every moment of my life.

So do you.

Hey, I said it was cheesy.

I realise none of this is what your mother and I talk about now, and that's what this letter was supposed to tell you, but it doesn't seem so relevant anymore. Maybe another time. I'm glad you know this. The things we talk about now, the things we wait until you're asleep to say, maybe one day they'll feel as quiet as the times I've just told you about and we'll be able to tell you, but for now I'll just leave them, right where they are.

I think it's time I put you to bed. I'll get your mother to do it with me. This has been a wonderful day.

Another one!

Love,
Dad

3/12/_____

What's so wonderful about that?

December 2nd _____

Dear Every,

You're a schoolgirl! Nearly two months now into reception. This is the first time we've brought your friends from school to our house for your birthday. The first time you've had 'friends from school'. You seem to have made a couple of them, though I suppose the process is somewhat less nuanced than it becomes. I don't suppose you'll know them anymore, much less remember them, so before I forget them too their names are Katie and Rebecca. They're the ones you seem to get along with best anyway. They're nice children. It's been great seeing you just be a child. I know I'm writing as much to the adult you'll be as to the child you are, and there aren't very many times when I remember to just watch you as you are. You're five years old, and today you've been laughing like someone who is, and that's how I've seen you. I now have an image burned deeply into my mind of you wearing a smudge of butter icing like a beard and laughing so loudly about it that it made Katie jump. My, how worries wane in the midst of sights like that one. In a very vague way I was almost tempted not to write this year, and to let that relief just exist on the day it did, but I didn't want it to go away. I think I'd have even photographed myself to catch it, if that was a reflex I possessed.

One of the other parents asked to see your baby pictures today. I think Rebecca's mum was just trying to be polite, but when I said we didn't have any, that we had never actually taken one, she looked at me like I'd missed out on something. She looked at you like you had too. Well, I'm sorry, but the only picture of you that I want to see is your face, the result of every picture anyone could have ever taken of you. I've missed out on the present too many times to miss out on yours. I've always been scared of the present, I think, because there are too many people I love whose presents I'm not in for me to think it anything good, but now I'm in yours, and I don't want to get any further from it than this paper is to the nib of my pen.

'Really? None?'

'Really. None.'

'Oh, we've got hundreds of Rebecca. At least. I'm trying to think if we've got one with Every in it.'

All the chatter in the room seemed to get sucked down a well when she said that.

'Maybe we have,' she said. 'I'm not sure.'

God, I hope not.

She turned away slowly, like she wasn't really trying to, and the thinking furrowed into her face. She sought out your mother, who turned and put her hand on Rebecca's mum's arm. Your mother had on a relaxed smile, which if I hadn't been so thrown, I'd have appreciated. She listened to something Rebecca's mum said and her face washed out, right around the eyes where the skin oldens first. 'No,' she said. Her mouth shaped the second sound slowly. She lifted her shoulders and tucked her elbows to her ribs. She cocked her head and let it roll back, spreading her lips out flat.

Rebecca's mum didn't talk to me for the rest of the afternoon. Neither did yours.

We've not yet got used to you not being here all day. The house seems like it's missing something when you're at school, and I swear that I can feel it just a little bit colder now that your body isn't warming it with ours. Leaving you at the classroom door for the first time was - how do I say it - odd, I suppose. Your teacher smiled at us in that oblivious teacher's way, and bless her, she doesn't know parenthood. She must be about the same age as your mother and I and that smile on her face marked how differently her life has gone from ours. Good for her. And she's good to you, you near enough love her. Miss Hatcher, that's her name, don't forget her. That first day you just wandered into the classroom like your life with us stopped at the door. We didn't get to say much of a goodbye, and I think we realise now how preposterous that concern was, I mean we saw you again in six hours. But what long hours they were. Sometimes I feel like they're still going on. Your mother and I were silent walking home. It was an enigmatic silence though, like we were a new couple again experiencing our first difficult day together, and in a way we were, because neither of us had ever done that before. We held hands for a moment here and there, but they were more touches than holds, and they didn't last. I realised as we turned onto our street that we hadn't walked home without you since nine months before you were born. It was like you weren't again. I'm not trying to liken it to a dead child because that's an awful thing to compare it to, and an awful thing full stop, but it was a loss, you know? At least it felt like one. Good lord, I hope I don't have a dead child. You know, I've never even thought about that, about you not being alive come your eighteenth or, this is horrible, your sixth, but we can't know things like that. I wish we couldn't think about things we can't know - why does it have to be that way? Well, I'm not going to let myself think about that, I just won't, but I will say that when you read this, and I'm happy to assume that you will, I hope you are okay. I just wish I wasn't so haunted by deaths that haven't happened yet.

Right, I was talking about being home without you, and I think I was poeticising it. I do promise to try not to do that, but I imagine there's very little chance of success. That's just me, Every, buried beneath my own graves of language - isn't that a horrible phrase? I wonder, if I never wrote a single word down, would you know me just as well? I guess we won't ever know. That would make all of this a waste. Well, forgive my language here my love, but it's a pretty fucking beautiful way to waste yourself, Every, and I'm fucking glad I'm doing it.

I can see myself writing more now that you are at school. Not more letters - well, not that I'd show you -

but just writing. Wasting, perhaps. It'll pass the time. It turns out six hours is a long time to pass. We drink a lot of tea now. Missing you is about all we do now, and picking you up again is like a new birth every day. Don't tell your mother I said that, because I imagine she might disagree, but heck, it's a nice feeling. That smile on your teacher's face makes a lot more sense to me now, and it somehow never fades. Your mother's kind of goes the other way. I feel bad too while you're gone, but for her it looks like you've had to be cut out of her each morning and she has to bleed all day until they put you back in. It doesn't seem to be getting any easier for her, but perhaps in time it will, and hopefully soon we can raise her to my level and we can both just be a little bit sad about it all day. It's not an awful sadness though, because there's a solace in there somewhere. It's that solace your mother is missing at the moment, and I'm not entirely sure where to find it for her. Or for you, when you'll need it one day.

To end on a happy note for this year, starting school has meant that a lot of people have asked about your name. I guess they still do! They always want to know where it comes from, and for some reason everyone expects you to know. All I say is that I liked the word. That I thought it sounded nice. Some people think so. Others don't. Your mother was unsure about it at first. On one of those days in the park that I told you about last year, she suggested maybe calling you Eve, which I admit I do like, but it just wasn't your name, so we ended up agreeing that we'd use it if either we wanted to or if other people gave us a hard enough time! But they haven't, and I'm glad about that. Every Hope - who would give you a hard time about being that?

Love as always,
Dad

3/12/_____

I don't actually like my name very much. Eve is nice.
Some people at school call me Eve.

Dear Every,

Last year your birthday was on a Sunday so we had you at home. This year it's on a Monday so you are at school and not here. You will be later, not long from now actually, and we have a mountain of presents for you and another of cake, but this is the first time I've written you a letter with you further than a doorframe away from me. Your heartbeat is playing where you are not. I can hear it very faintly.

I think this year has produced the first memory of your life that won't go away. You seem about the right age. Thankfully it's a happy one if it's what I think it is, but I guess there's always the danger that I'm wrong. That is for you to know.

In the summer we took you to a small beach near Dorset. Hopefully you're thinking of it now, and smiling, but it's for you to tell me how much like the real thing your memory of it is. If it's like any other memory it probably won't be a lot. I'm going to tell you about that day, but you go right on and remember it your way, Every. Don't change a memory on the truth's account.

I had been there before, years ago and accidentally, with your mother. I think I had known her for about a year. We didn't yet live together and although we had been away for the weekend a few times, it was the furthest away we had gone. We stayed in a small cottage about a mile from the coast. It had large windows looking out over the fields. It was motionless out there, except for a narrow road a few hundred yards inland. Every few minutes a car would drift along it, reminding us we weren't as far out of the way as it seemed. We could hear the cars for a few seconds after they disappeared.

There were some leaflets left out on the coffee table. Somewhere nearby there was an old mine, but your mother saw the one about the coastal path and so that was all she wanted to do.

She really likes the water.

We had been walking for a few hours. It was a lot of hills and some steps here and there and some ice cream in between. We were between villages where the bays stop having names. I never worked out why there were wooden gates every few minutes, but your mother got into the habit of climbing up and trying to balance on them. Like we weren't high up enough already. And sometimes she would gaze down and sometimes she would close her eyes but every time she would try and balance on the very top of the gate. She didn't fall. Thank God she didn't fall.

I'd lost count of how many gates we'd passed through when the path opened out into a wide slope that steepened and then levelled out. Then after a bend, the bay appeared. 'Whoa,' I said, and your mother said something similar. We'd seen coves before. We were beach people. But it was a thin shore, with rocks outstretched at the far side towards a mound, like an arm to its hand. And the hand was open. And it was inviting us. I wondered if you could walk to it when the tide was out, but the tide was not out and instead the waves broke sharply. We looked for a way down. The cliff beneath us was sheer and we couldn't see a path on our side or on any other. 'Let's go round,' your mother said to me. I followed her. It was just after a small footbridge that we saw the beginnings of a footway hidden amongst the thornbushes. It must have been hacked out by walkers. Your mother pushed part of the bush back and then stepped in front of it to hold it. She looked at her hand. The thorns hadn't cut her, but I couldn't tell from her face whether she was okay with that or not. 'Go through,' she said.

The path was so narrow and loose that it looked like we would be walking down a cliff on a string. I wanted to say, 'No, I don't want to,' but I agreed. I always agree.

The days before had been dry and the dirt on the path was loose. The path meandered, and every time I had to turn, my foot slipped towards the edge. It was only inches away to begin with. The path was maybe a foot wide and the fall beneath it long. You'd step and you'd kick a rock out. I'd be surprised if someone hasn't been hurt there. I've no idea how many times I asked your mother if she was okay. She always was. She asked me too, and I lied.

The path ended about fifteen feet above the sand. There was a sheet of dark grey rock between the beach and us, and it wasn't far off vertical. I was breathing hard enough that I noticed it. Your mother placed one foot against the rockface and started shifting her weight back and forth. I told her to be careful. I sat down and eyed a few protruding rocks to use as footholds. I slid down, and I caught myself on the footholds, and it wasn't a graceful descent but I got there. I looked back to check on your mother. She still had her foot over the edge, and she bent at the knees and put one hand on the ground, and she tried to slide down on just her feet. She tripped almost immediately and tumbled on her side, recoiling off the footholds, and she landed at the bottom in a heap. I nearly hit that spot before she did. She said, 'I'm okay,' as soon as she realised I was hovering over her, and I think I shouted at her. Something about there being no one there to help us if she got hurt. 'It's quicker than how you did it,' she said. 'I'm fine.' Her leg was bleeding in scattered scratches. I think it was from the thornbush.

We were alone there. We looked around. In one direction it was all sea, glistening and rugged, and in the other it was just cliffside and waterfall. From down there it seemed that there was more beach than we had seen from the path, but it was still only us. The world may as well have been gone. We took a walk along the sand, holding hands, and mine was colder than hers. The sound of the sea echoed off the cliff face into one cacophonous rumble. We left our t-shirts and our shoes on a rock about the size of a table. How convenient was that.

'I like it here,' your mother said to me.

I did not agree, but I did not say so. We walked to the water. I went in a few steps at a time but your mother was waist deep in seconds, and she was maybe ten feet ahead of me. 'Come on,' she said.

Well, I did my best. Your mother dunked her head and I, well, to tell you the truth, I don't much like getting my hair wet. I hobbled my way out to her, each freezing wave straightening me up until it ebbed away. The sea lapped at me, and your mother laughed at me. I watched her lean back, and then she turned, smiling thinly, and she swam.

I do not take my eyes off of her when she swims.

I tracked her head as it bobbed between waves, and I checked every possible place she could emerge from when she dipped her head below. It got smaller as she went further, of course it did, and eventually I felt myself taking steps forwards. Her head became indistinguishable from the shine on the peaks of the waves. Suddenly the water didn't feel so cold anymore.

I suppose she wasn't gone long, but seconds turn into minutes and minutes transcend time. When she appeared she was much closer than when I had lost sight of her, and then she was close enough to me to walk instead of swim.

'That was lovely,' she said.

'I couldn't see you.'

'I'm fine.'

'But I couldn't see you.'

She looked at me through the salt in her eyes, and her shoulders lapsed forwards as she breathed out, as though looking at me was too much work. And who knows, maybe it was. Maybe it is.

'Will you come with me?' she asked. 'Over there?' She turned to look at the mound at the end of the rocks.

I nodded. I didn't want to speak because I didn't want to lie to her.

She started to swim and I fell onto the water too. I swam with my face on the surface, which made it hard to keep up and harder to see her and I tried not to think about the point at which my feet would no longer touch the bottom, but I guess you know full well what happens when you try not to think about something. I could make out ahead of me that your mother was on the shore, and that made the swim easier, I think. And really, it wasn't very far. My arms and my knees hit the sand and I stood and walked the rest of the way.

As I got near to her, I could see that her feet were starting to bleed from several long, jagged scratches. I guess the water had rinsed it away until she got out.

'What happened?' I asked.

I knew what had happened.

'I must have caught myself on something.'

There must have been a dozen cuts.

It strikes me now that I am writing this, that it is possible that I shouldn't be, that you shouldn't know this about her, and that you don't need to know that she's the kind of person who scrapes her feet across the sea floor to cut them. Apparently I don't feel strongly enough about that to stop, but I guess I have however many years to change my mind, or to admit that my mind says what it does, and to not show you this. We will have to see.

My jaw stiffened and shook, and my arms followed. I felt my neck widen as it started to shiver too and then my chest tightened as the skin on it shivered along with the rest. I had only swum for seconds, but I guess I don't do so well in the cold. Even still, sunlight piled down on us like a weight, and it was warm on the mound. There was a rock just ahead of me that was right under the sun, and I stepped towards it, shaking all the way. I turned and rested against it. I could feel the heat against my back and my skin sank into it, but my jaw and my chest and most of me really kept quivering and gnawing and writhing. Your mother stood and watched me while she bled onto the sand.

And then it passed.

We stayed there a while. I warmed up and the sand clotted into your mother's feet. When we went back, I climbed over the rocks and your mother took to the water. The walk back up to the path wasn't much better than the trip down.

It was in the spring of this year that your mother started talking about the beach again. I guess she didn't before because she knew I hadn't liked it. It started as discreet allusions, like when she said the seagulls reminded her of the coast. Then it was several trips to the seaside in a week, and making sure I knew how much you had liked making sandcastles. But I suspect it was a wasted effort. I suppose it was tactful, but she only had to say it and I would have agreed. I always agree.

It occurs to me that I don't think we told you where we were taking you. Perhaps we meant it as a surprise. It is strange to me that I have forgotten. I don't often forget. But I do remember you wanted strawberry ice cream at the stop before the cove, and that it was so warm outside you had to drink half of it out of the cone. Oh well. You walked close to your mother when we got going again, and your mother walked close to me, and when we got to the wooden gates she kept one foot in front of the other and just passed on through. She put your hand in mine at the thornbush.

The walk down didn't phase you. At least it didn't look like it did. I was worried each time my foot slipped that my arm would rip yours forwards, but my foot never did much more than a stutter and a pause, and I am wondering now that I am writing it how much of the danger of the walk down has been overstated by my memory. Memories do that, you see.

Your mother walked ahead of us, and I watched her closely. My memory didn't overstate that concern, I know it. Her steps were small, and slow, and as she went on she turned her head to check that you were okay.

'Are you okay, Every?'

You said, 'Yes,' and you said it every time. You enunciate very well.

We made it as far as the drop to the sand, and I don't think we'd really thought that part through. 'I'll go down first,' I said. I stumbled down much as I did before. Looking back up at you and your mother, it seemed a lot higher. Your mother held your hand and you steadied yourself on one of the footholds, and then I reached up and eased you down to the beach. I let you go and you dusted yourself off while I looked back up and saw your mother looking straight at me. I took a step to the side to get under her. She put both hands on the precipice and lowered herself to a foothold.

'Have you got me?' she asked.

I nodded and I held my arms up. She slid into them and down to the shore.

'Okay?' I said.

'Okay.'

The three of us walked towards the water. I looked all around to see if anyone else was there but we were alone. Up on one of the other cliffsides someone was giving up getting down. We left our things on the rock and walked to the shoreline, dipping our feet into the sea. It was not as cold as I remember it being before. You ran off ahead of us and splashed seawater back with your heels. It was delightfully irritating.

'You go with her,' your mother said to me. 'I'm going to swim. Don't worry, I won't go far.'

I let her go. I still don't know how to tell if that was the right decision, but then I don't suppose it was mine to make. She waded out up to her knees. I thought, 'That's far enough,' and for that I don't forgive myself. I don't forgive myself for anything.

I called out to you. 'Have you seen that?' I pointed to the waterfall, tucked away by itself, running endlessly for no one but itself.

'Oh,' you said - more like yelped.

I knew you'd like it. You ran ahead to it. I did follow, but I did so still staring at your mother. She must have felt my eyes at her back. She had not moved much, and she did not move much more before I was closer to you than to her. I went with you to the waterfall, and our voices loudened the nearer we got. You held your hands under it. 'Do you want to go in?' I asked. The stream coming from it was shallow enough. You stepped into it without answering. No need, I suppose. I sat just in front of you on the edge of a rock.

Your mother was swimming maybe thirty feet out.

'Oh!' you shouted again across the span of a few seconds. Your voice rose like you were singing. The water whitened as it hit you. Then you sat in the middle of the stream under the fall. The water shot from you to me. You laughed and I laughed.

It was hard to make out where your mother was from behind the spray, but I could do it, just about. She was walking back to the shore. I was thankful. She called out,

'Come here,' with a smile as wide as her outstretched arms. You started shuffling to get out and you posted an arm on my shoulder to lift yourself up. You walked off and I turned to get out. Your steps left behind some wet footprints and, once they had dried, one of your feet left blood drops behind them instead. I didn't even think that much of it.

'You want to help me, Every?' You and your mother spelled out some words with pebbles. I couldn't read them from where I was. It took you a few minutes, and then your mother took you down to the water. I followed. I read what you had written: No one knows we're here.

I went down to the shore and as far out as where the water touched my waist. Your mother held you and you tried to swim. You took to the water like, well, a little girl. Your mother did not let go.

'Can we go over there?' you asked, looking at the mound by the rocks.

Your mother looked. Then she said, 'No, it's too far.' The tide was in and over some of the rocks too.

You carried on swimming. I carried on watching.

You swam for a few minutes, then you played kicking water at each other, and then you played kicking water at me. I'll admit it, I played my own game of walking off grumpily. Don't worry, I got over it.

When you joined me back on the shore, your mother had you by the hand. You read your words back - you are quite good at reading, you really are. And as you read them out, I heard that they were a good thing. I have to admit that when I saw them first, I was not so sure. Your mother took you over to the waterfall and rinsed you off in it. As she did, I looked out to the mound. I saw the rock I had shivered on. Your mother was right that we couldn't take you over there that day, but I'll take you back there when you're a stronger swimmer. And then that old, imagined apparition of myself will watch for you to make it over the tide, and when you get over to him, and you lay your hand where he was, the last of those shivers will give in to the warmth of your skin. And your mother and I will both appreciate it, because we've been waiting.

Love,
Dad

3/12/_____

That's exactly how I remember it.

Dear Every,

The solace (I remember using that word) that I wanted to help your mother find, she seems to have found for herself. She's either found a real peace or given up on one completely. Nothing seems to frighten her anymore. But there are ways you look at her that show me it's frightening you, like the way you purse your lips when she holds her side. I don't even understand how you know, but I guess you know your own mother's body and you can tell when it's going away. She doesn't look that different, it's just that the wasting that's been going inside her for however long is starting to come out, like she's filled herself with so much withering now that it's gripping at her skin because there's not enough left beneath it. It just makes her look tired. And she is tired.

She used to talk - these conversations did not take place in parks as far as I can remember, they seem far more suited to cold kitchens - she used to talk about whether she was someone who maybe shouldn't have children. I thought she was being down on herself, and I always told her it wasn't true. And I was being selfish, yes, I admit that, because I wanted you. She was always worried that you would take after her too much, that there's a tendency towards her old kind of life and you would copy it if you saw it, but you haven't seen it, because you cured everything for her. Just not everything

65

in her, because there is damage there that is out of your hands and that was only ever in hers. We always knew that she had hurt herself enough that it would come out before too long, and I know now what those cold kitchen conversations were about: she didn't want to die. She didn't want to have you knowing she had taken herself out of your life before it started. But the fact remains that she may have. It was a choice she made, over and over again with each handful of tablets, and I only wish she could have another chance to make those choices now that she knows how real you would become. It eats at her, and it doesn't help. I tell her to sleep, but I think she's had enough of it. Suddenly every sleepless night we had when you were in a cradle is a time she got to spend awake with you, and that's all she wants to do now. You both enjoy it, even if you both know what it really is. It is quiet time. There is never much laughter, although don't take that to mean there's sadness because there isn't, and sometimes you just sit with each other. Sometimes you just lay with your head on her belly, and sometimes she lays her head on yours. I've always found a unity in silence and my god this is one united family. I feel bad when I join you because part of me feels that that time is not for me, but I see your mother's eyes open towards me like sunrises, and then I know, and then I believe, that she wants me there as well. Two sunrises at the same time. If they weren't going to burn each other out I'd say I was the most fortunate person to ever walk under a sun.

Look, she has never been good to herself, Every, and I don't know how much of this year she'll have with you. There are two abscesses on her liver and the doctor says she has given herself toxic hepatitis. It is bad enough that her liver is failing. She used to just live with it, with a stabbing pain in the top of her stomach, but because she just kept on hurting it more, the damage is irreversible. It will kill her, we have been told, without a transplant. And the chances of that are not exactly in our favour. But who knows, maybe we're wrong, maybe the doctors are too, and maybe we're still all together. But maybe we're right, and accepting it is all we can do, and accepting that she's fading from my past as much as my present is all I can do. My life up until now seems a lot lonelier, and the Sunday afternoons we all waste together are the only ones that are not lonely, and I wonder, as she fades from my memories little by little, how many memories there are left to make. And that by the nature of a mind, I am already losing, and have been losing all along, my memories of her. I hope those times exist alone, right where they were, and that we both appreciate them even when we don't know about them anymore. And I hope that the time you have left with your mother yields a thousand embraces so that when you start to forget them, as you will as soon as she lets go of the first one, you can make at least one of them last forever. She is too tired to make one last forever herself - even she has to sleep. I watch her go to sleep often, and the way she falls into it has changed. There is an exhaustion I cannot fathom. I don't know what I'm seeing, but it's the same thing I've started to see on your face when I put you to bed. Something's happening to both of you - in both of you - and it's not happening to me.

I love you both,
Dad

3/12/_____

I remember Mum being ill but she still looked really pretty.

December 2nd _____

Dear Every,

I shouldn't be doing this. She's in the next room, you are too, and she is still here. It's dark in there because of her eyes. They can't take in a lot more, you see, so we keep it vigil-dim in there and I came in here to write to you. The door is slightly ajar. There are only a few hours left of your birthday, and I'm sorry it hasn't been a happy one, but I think your mother wanted to see just one more. I hope she sees all of it - I'd hate for your birthday to be the last day she lived. We were at the hospital today. It was the same as always. They gave her pain relief and told her what's best, but all she wanted to do was to be at home. Here we are.

I've heard about people being able to decide when to die. My grandfather buried his mother when he was old himself, and she died on her own mother's birthday. She told him she would do that. Good for her. I believe your mother has chosen to die after yours. We'll see when.

She barely speaks anymore. She just can't. It's strange to think I may have heard her voice for the last time, and I don't think I really believe it yet. I can't remember what it was she said last. Probably nothing much. I didn't know the significance of it, I promise I didn't, and I'll miss it, whatever it was, forever. I used to hear significance in everything she said. I don't know what happened to change that and I certainly never loved her any less, but I promise I will hear anything she has left to say. Her silence is as beguiling as song. I'll try to treasure it while it's here. Will it go with her? There's another unanswerable question I never even needed to think of. Damn it, just damn it.

All she does is breathe. I don't see the point. I don't know what our lives are, Every, but I can see a breathing body for what it is and it isn't enough. God, you know everything now, don't you? What happened to our lives, Every? She lies there, I watch her, and I make secret wishes that each heaving of her stomach will be the last, but even if they get shallower and I call you in so we can watch her go together, she floods her lungs just full enough to survive a little longer. I guess it's to be admired. Maybe some time that's what I'll do.

I'm trying not to think of what you're seeing in there right now, but that imagination I used to wonder about is really starting to kick in. Watching death seems to do that to people. I'm imagining you in the chair by the bed, the lamplight filling the scar on your chin. You are calm, just watching. Your stomach goes in and out with your mother's and you do it on purpose. And you try to do the same with your hearts. Your mother's heart beats slower than yours, and you touch her chest and wait for them to beat exactly in time with one another. Just once. Even if it's only for a beat it's enough. And I imagine some reaction in her at the moment it happens - a dilated pupil, a decibel of breath - so that you both know. Then your hearts go off in their own directions and wait for it to happen once more. You hope that it will, but you can't know.

I just looked into the room. It's dark in there but I could see you. You are asleep and with any luck you'll stay that way. Your mother is too. I know she's still there because I can hear her breath from across the room now. I've trained myself to it. You are on the bed with her, curled up to her, and she is lying flat but I can tell from the creases in the covers that she tried to curl up too. I'll leave you alone for now. I'll sit here for a while and let you two be together and you don't need me for that. And then later I will join you. I'll lie on the bed as quietly as I can, and I'll listen to her breath. And yours. I already know how similar they sound, and it doesn't surprise me because really it's all the same breath isn't it? Everything happens in the same one and we pant our own ways through it, exhausted. But I'll listen to it, and I'll touch both your hearts, their skin bindings at least, and I won't be surprised when they don't stop beating in time with each other. And then after I smile thinly, it will upset me, because your mother's heart is about to stop and I don't know what will happen to yours.

Nor, oh god, mine.

3/12/_____

Don't be scared Dad. Please don't be.

December 2nd _____

Dear Every,

This is how I remember it.

Your mother had two more days after your eighth birthday, they were long ones for us all, and I think she had them because she wasn't ready when she thought she would be. But I think I didn't help. I turned on the recording of your heart - I thought she'd want to believe she was taking it with her - and I think every time she was nearly ready, it pulled her right back out of it. How vicious. But if I dragged death out for her then so be it, because you know what, she died to the sound of you, to the happiest day of her life, and even though it worries me to think I prolonged her suffering, I'm sure she didn't mind. I'm not crying at that thought and I don't understand why. God knows I cry at a lot of others.

You hadn't left the room for a few hours before I played the recording, and when it started, you asked me what it was. 'It's you,' I said, and it looked like you turned cold inside, like the ghost of your newborn self was filling you and freezing you. What does that even mean? You're too young to tell me and I'm too old to know. Twenty eight years old and a widower. That word sounds like a synonym for Old Man. I don't think that's going to change.

Your mother was adamant that she wanted to die at home. A nurse visited us twice a day in the last few weeks.

She gave your mother painkillers, although they didn't seem to do all that much. And your mother wanted to feel it, at least a little. I don't understand that. I don't understand that at all. For all the love I have for her, for all the sacrifices she has made, she brought this death on herself. She knew that and I don't feel bad saying it anymore. But I do wonder if I should feel bad for letting her die the way she did. I've gone over it in my head so many times now that I can't tell if allowing it was the mark of my love for her, or my ultimate failing of her. I won't know, will I? Ever. That's okay. There are some things we think about that are sacred to our hearts. Let's not spoil them by solving them.

But surely she had felt enough of a death? Surely the feeling of her body eating at itself was enough? Well, I suppose not. It's upsetting to me that she couldn't share those feelings with me, that I couldn't take just a few of them from her, but I think that was the point of it - that she could absorb everything she had taken on throughout her life. There were plenty of happinesses in it, don't forget that, but there was a lot of, I suppose, exposure, too. Part of me wishes her body had been naked when she went, I think it would have been the most exposed way for her to go, but it wasn't. It? What am I saying? I don't know, Every, but I had to watch that damn body do things I've never seen it do, and I stopped seeing it as her at all anymore. It heaved so much. I didn't know a chest could move like that. And the sounds she made got louder. Thinner, too, like she was screaming her way into suffocation. She couldn't cry, I don't think. Her eyes were dry, too dry to be a person's, but you and I had enough tears for three between us. We could have washed her in our tears, and maybe we should have. No, of course not. That's just the kind of poetic thought you need to avoid, Every. Don't think like me. And don't remember like me either. As I am writing this, I wish you were old enough for me to be sure that the memories you have of your mother before she died will stay with you, because I don't want her death - you watched it all, you brave soul - to be all you have of her. I fear it won't be long before it's all I have. It might be already. Don't remember like me, Every, just don't. It's confusing to think that any new image I get of her will be imagination. Hell, there are things I remember about her now that probably never happened, though of course I couldn't say what. I'm losing her. I'm creating her. What a space to fill.

We watched her together for hours, in silence except for our eerie breathing, and when they finally took her away, we shared the bed. I did not change the sheets. We could smell her, or the smells that had become her, and you asked me where she was. You still do even though every smell of hers is gone. I should know, because I've dragged my nose around the house a whole hopeless night at a time trying to find one. There might be one I've never actually smelled, I suppose, and I wish. She could be hidden somewhere in plain sight - in a candle, say -

engulfing us and our house with herself, keeping us warm, but staying anonymous. I doubt it, but it's nice to think that way.

You have never asked me when she'll come back, not even at her funeral, which was your first. Forget it happened. Let's do that together. Let's do that for each other.

That is how I remember it.

Happy birthday, Every.

There are balloons in the kitchen and a cake by the stairs. Your friends from school won't be over today - we will be alone. So for now, I'm going to call you downstairs, and you'll see the cake, and I'll tell you it's your birthday because you stopped remembering it two days short of a year ago. We will smile and I'll play with you and I'll give you your presents, and then you will ask me where she is because there are none from her. We will both miss her when I don't answer, but really they are all from her, and it will still be your birthday, and I'll be damned if you don't go to bed happy.

You are loved no less without her.

Love,
Your father, and, I know,
Your mother

3/12_____

I remember what it sounded like. It sounds like dying hurts.

December 2nd _____

Dear Every,

This is how I remember it.

Each spring I waited for the folk music festival that came to town late in May. I didn't often listen to music at home because I always liked watching people play their songs, and this was before you could do that all day on the computer. I'd wait all year to hear songs I didn't know, sung by strangers. I find it captivating. The festival was in the park, and I remember walking through the gardens, hearing snippets of songs as I went past each of the stages, like banners out the front of a shop, and I wished so badly that I could find a spot to stand in where I could hear it all perfectly, but if that spot existed somewhere, I never found it. It's interesting what you find yourself drawn to when you're surrounded by things you want. I found myself drifting towards a white marquee. There was a band out the front playing some traditional sounding song, and they were doing a fine job of it too, but the closer I got, the more a thin, whispering voice misted the air at the marquee entrance. I hadn't even heard it from out in the park, but I was glad I came across it when I did.

And no, it wasn't your mother singing. As a matter of fact I always loved her voice, it was rasping and low like the old jazz croons, but I only ever heard it when she didn't know I was there. And then she would see me, and she would blush, and I would tell her that it was nice, and then she would go back to whatever else she was doing. But there was no way she'd ever sing in front of people - or do anything else in front of them to be honest - if she could avoid it. That was a shame. Yes, it was certainly a shame.

It was warmer inside the marquee than I had expected. The heat barricaded the entrance and I had to trawl through it to get in. The voice inside was welcoming to me. It came from a small man, sat on a stool, playing a parlour guitar and singing about living on the streets. I don't know if he did live on the streets, but he had a voice so hushed that I'd believe it. So hushed it was almost absent. And still, it was the most enthralling thing there. Well, that's a lie, because your mother was there too.

I didn't find her immediately. The entrance was head on with the stage and ahead of me was a group of people huddled near it, with a few others dotted around the space where they could either listen privately or not at all. Two people were having a conversation, which I thought was rude. It wasn't crowded. I went towards the group at the front, and I went towards them quietly because the music was so quiet even a footstep could impede. I stood behind them. I listened for a good fifteen minutes before I went to back up and realised the crowd had grown, and that it had halfway filled the marquee. I wondered where on earth all those people had come from. There was no sign telling us who he was, no flashing lights outside saying something was happening there. Just a man's voice drifting through the rests in the traditional band's playing. But I guess that's how the world tends to do things. It doesn't sound an alarm every time something is about to happen to you and it doesn't leave a trail so that you end up where you should. Mind you, the help wouldn't go amiss sometimes.

The man played for another five, ten minutes. To be honest, it didn't really look like he was enjoying himself. He looked down a lot and he sighed between songs. But it sounded good, and I wish there had been a chance to tell him that. I worked my way to the back of the crowd so I could leave quickly afterwards and get to another stage, and as I lingered by the entrance I noticed someone else was there too. She had her head down, and she was swaying with movements as slight as the singer's voice. And she always moved that way, until a year ago, when she died. There may not have been an alarm that day, but that man's voice was enough. I never found out who he was, but I'm glad he was there.

That is how I remember it.

There are balloons in the kitchen and a cake by the stairs. Your friends from school won't be over today - we will be alone. So for now I'm going to call you downstairs, and you'll see the cake, and we will smile and I'll play with you and give you your presents - they say they're from Mum and Dad - and you will tell me that's wrong. We will both miss her when I don't answer, but I promise they are all from her - everything is - and it will still be your birthday and I'll be damned if you don't somehow go to bed happy.

You are loved no less without her. Happy birthday, Every.

Love,
Your father, and, I know,
Your mother

3/12/_____

?

Dear Eleanor,

I have spent the day in the cold. I don't know which of those letters I'll give to Every, but I said in one of them that you could be in a candle, and that has stayed with me. So the only heat in this house today is coming from candles - maybe twenty of them, thirty of them - and I am waiting for some semblance of warmth to come over me so I can feel you here again. I have chosen to believe that it will bring you here again.

Every has cried, finally. She is crying now. She is cold. She didn't cry when you died, but when they took your body I could see the tears coming the same way your smiles used to. If she did cry, she didn't do it around me, and that's quite the grasp of privacy for someone her age, though I'm not sure if it's hers she's grasped or mine. But the cold has brought it out of her, and once this day has passed its way back to you I'll put the heat back on again. Then we'll exist without the cold of winter until it isn't winter anymore. We'll exist without what winter is, isn't that wrong? Next year I might do this again, for no other reason than I want you here. And there's solace in this cold. There's solace in waiting if you don't expect it ever to end.

Every's crying is quietening - I think she is nearing sleep. I am on the way myself, and I have just turned on the recording of her heart. I'll fall asleep to it like we used to. I fell asleep to it the other night too, on Every's birthday. She came into our bedroom (I'll always call it ours) and she asked me what that sound was. I guess she had forgotten. I told her it was you. And she climbed into bed and cuddled up to me and went to sleep happy.

Tonight I'll dream it is you.

3/12/_____

I'm crying louder now Dad. I hope you can hear me because it's your fault.

Dear Every,

I've always been convinced that a father is not all that much and now that's all you've had for the best part of two years. I have been collecting your mother's post and keeping it aside, as though she might come back for it. It is in two piles in the study: the pile that only has her name on it and the pile that has mine on it too. Her pile was larger to begin with. I never really appreciated how many things we had only put in her name. I kept an eye on the return addresses as the post came through, and I added the things I recognised to the shared pile. Credit cards, mailing lists, something about the TV license. When I saw the same address more than a couple of times, I opened it, and usually, it turned out I should have opened it sooner. We've never had the power cut off or anything, but we have skirted a little too close to that from time to time. And your mother was due her eye test. They're going to charge her anyway. Let them.

My pile grew as the obligations stacked up. At least I have a better idea of what needs doing around here. A new letter is added to your mother's pile about once every few weeks, usually around the end of the month. I often wonder what is in them. Did she have investments? Had she applied for jobs? Is there a friend I don't know about? Probably not. She'd have told me. But keeping them sealed keeps the thought alive. Better a thought than nothing. I have hovered a pen over the faces of the envelopes a couple of times now:

NO LONGER AT THIS ADDRESS.

RETURN TO SENDER.

DECEASED.

HELP.

But as yet, they sit blank, and on the side.

The time you are at school is time I have been able to practise being a parent. There are very few dinners I have made for you that I didn't first try at lunch that day. And most of the times I have settled for giving you oven chips are the times I couldn't get a lasagne or a chilli to come out right. They are not supposed to be difficult. I can't imagine what the neighbours think seeing me barbequing sausages at eleven a.m. on a Tuesday. Well, they've never said anything. We eat a lot of mashed potato in the holidays.

By the time you come home the smell of the herbs and oils has either dissipated or it has blended into the evening. The sound of the key in the door masks the wiping away of whatever tears I was permitted that day, and I rub them hard into my jeans as I stand to greet you.

You always say Hello. I always try my best to. The days I can tell you that dinner is in the oven are my favourites.

Today we had moussaka.

3/12/_____

I liked it.

Dear Eleanor,

This cold is the only way I hear Every cry now. Her crying is a lot like yours. I can only remember you crying a few times after she was born. God, there were so many times before that, weren't there? I hear all of them again in Every's whimpers, and every tear must break into mirrors of every time you ever had one. She tells me 'It's cold' and I tell her 'I know' and I light a candle and tell her to hold it near her face. She holds it near her skin and I tell her you are in it. Then she looks at me over the top of the flame. And her eyes scrunch up, and tears the flame can't evaporate because, really, the heat almost isn't there, fall out of them. I know it's not the cold making her cry, it's the thinking of you, but while she's in that cold Every shows me what she doesn't all year. I don't know why I worship that sadness but there's something in it that's not in her smile. She blows out the candle and her white breath shows its face - your face - in the last of the candleglow. If only it showed itself when we breathed in too. There's a lot of exhaling in the cold left to do, and a lot of breath to lose trying to find you. It might feel like we're suffocating, but we sit for warmth in each other's arms and breathe out all we can and the sound she hears is the heart she thinks is you. Together our dead breath makes a portrait of you and the three of us are together again.

3/12/_____

It hurts in the cold. I wish it was cold more.

Dear Every,

This year we waited for winter together. Neither of us said we wanted it so badly but when it came I saw you'd been waiting just as patiently and as secretly as I was. The slowness of your movements through the long summer made sense to me. You didn't want to disturb the air for fear of warming it up and postponing the first freeze, of having your existence in the world change its course. You hardly played at all, or screamed or laughed, or did anything that might alert the world to you, but you can't be invisible to the world you're in, Every, not to the sun. It sees everything and it's seen it all. But winter came just this morning, or at least its symptoms did, and you existed again as you wanted to, in a world that was the way you wanted it to be. That's a lucky thing, Every. An eclipse is more common.

You shouldn't really look into either.

I saw your relief at it coming this morning too, like a moon across a star, in the crescent of your mouth on your face. It wasn't the happiest of smiles - you seem to have outgrown those already at eleven. And that beats even your mother, if my timelines are correct. But it was the smile of someone who had finally seen what they had spent too long waiting for, and that's a kind with a mercy on the one who sees it, and one on the person blessed with it so bless it. Some people spend longer looking for that than your whole lifetime has lasted - isn't that awful? I am not one of those people. I know that. And I know that makes me fortunate.

You awoke this morning before me. If there's one thing you've not outgrown it's waking early on your birthday. It was cold when I woke. I could feel it from under the covers. I walked downstairs and found you in the kitchen, barefoot on the floor. At least it wasn't stone. Before I could pull a Happy Birthday from somewhere inside myself and before I could give you your card, you turned that smile towards me and suddenly I felt that dreadful cold on my throat and I swear I'd have cut right through it to stop it.

'Every, your feet,' I said instead, and you said, 'Look.'

You breathed out hard so that you could show me something. You'd been waiting nearly a year to see your breath inside and there it was, fleeting and white, its residue disappearing as soon as you closed your mouth. You snapped it shut like you had only so much air to spill, which, now that I think about it, we all do. How many breaths do we have left? Every one of us would lose count, and we'd lose our lives to trying if we tried. Your lips hit one another like a clasp. All I could say was, 'I know,' because I did. But there are only a couple of days before that cold is right back where it should be, and although it is beautiful we can't do it to ourselves every day, so we have to wait. We should wait. That's why it is warm inside now. It is warm inside and so you are not. It is a slow morning and I am watching you play, or I am watching you pretend to, from the kitchen window, and I am writing while I do.

Maybe if there was snow this wouldn't look so damn sad to me. There would be a snowman, or snowballs if there wasn't enough of it, and you'd run around like all children do in the snow. The joy I'd see would make the breath coming out of you something other than the only reason you were out there, which of course it would be, and, of course, it is. A child's smile can make any pain go away, though maybe not their own. Well, as far as the parent who's watching them can see anyway. I wish that was what I was looking at. You're in the same red coat you'd be in if it were snowing, under the same hat with the fluffy balls hanging off the side of it, but the blanketed ground and its inherent joy are not there with you. You are in the garden, away from the trees (we've an apple and a pear tree, I hope they are still there) and you are kicking the ground like you would if there were dandelions on it, but there are not. You're trying to look like you want to be out there, but all you're doing is following your breath around. There's so much of it, I can see it from in here. You're looking at it floating away like it was a dancing cloud, but for goodness' sake, Every, it is not. Putting that coat on you this morning was the hardest thing. I should have kept you in but as the house warmed that smile of yours fell away and I couldn't be the reason it went. It had been a while since I'd seen one. I zipped your coat up for you, my knee touching the floor, and you looked me in the eye like you were looking at nothing: I am not the one you want. I know that. So letting you go outside is all I could think of to do. Your breath, your mother's ghost as perhaps you think of it, isn't lingering between our walls today, it is leaving you as soon as you breathe it, and I think you are beginning to understand that. You are chasing it. It won't work, Every. God, watching you try is killing me now. We buried all we had of her already. I have to get you in.

You're in. I thought you'd try and stop me, but you took my hand when I held it out for you. You looked at my face and I saw the only reason you weren't crying was that the tears had frozen into your eyelashes. Oh, Every, does grieving never end? I hope it does and I hope it has. Tell me it has, even if it's a lie, please. We walked inside and I saw you breathe out slow and long and watch it stray behind you, and I shut the door. It was warm. We were sad. She's coming again in a couple of days, Every. It's too long for you to wait, isn't it? You just went upstairs and the heartbeat is playing in your room. I'll leave it with you.

I'm alone downstairs again, and I doubt I'll see you until lunch. I have a present, a diary that I hope you'll keep with you but always leave blank, but to tell you the truth we both forgot it was your birthday when you said 'Look.' I'll give it to you later, when you have had some time. For now I'll keep myself company with the gift you gave me. You came inside and when you thought I wasn't looking you climbed onto the table and breathed onto the window. You looked at it like it was a portrait of your mother, and in that moment I admit I wished there was a photo of her I could have shown you, but there is not. You know that, though, and you took your thawing finger and wrote her name in your breath. I hung your coat up, felt my heart beat too hard, and you walked silently past me up the stairs and into your room. I hurried before your breath faded away. I didn't want it to, I'll never want it to, and watching her name disappear with it brought me tears I couldn't cry. My eyes were so close to her again. Thank you, Every. It's so fucking painful but thank you. If she could see us now she wouldn't believe in god anymore, even if she's with him, because looking at this, there's nothing here to believe in.

Love,
Dad

3/12/_____

I can remember writing in the window. If you look hard you can still see her name in it. Actually you don't have to look very hard.

I do write in the diary. Sorry. I thought that was what it was for. These notes are in my diary actually.

I'll tear them all out one day.

Dear Eleanor,

I am writing this in our bed on a cold morning. I never meant to see you in frozen breath but Every does and now I do too. I'm under the covers, and I am warm and comfortable like I haven't been in years because it is cold enough to make it so that you are here with me. There is almost no use for a candle anymore but I'll light some when I'm finished writing so that Every will see that today is special. She is still asleep. I wanted to write before she woke up because I know that everything I do after that will be a mistake, so this is the one right thing I will do today. I realise now that I have sanctified this day so much that I am trapped writing to you now too. And I realised as I wrote that sentence that I consider all of these letters to be things that trap me. They didn't start out that way, which you know. I feel trapped by the knowledge that Every will read hers and hate them and everything that went into them, even though I know she doesn't have to read a single word or know that one was ever written. And I feel trapped, too, by the knowledge that you won't.

When I think about my life with you, I feel like these memories are someone else's. I watch them, photographs never taken. There you are with the crows feet besides your eyes, but the me in them doesn't look like me or anyone I ever was. I don't know what Every sees, and I don't honestly know why she would look. She misses you, what would be the point? What a waste of three words, of course she misses you.

I've forgotten why you dyed your hair. It was only a little darker than usual, still blonde, and I think it was before our wedding that you started doing it. Your eyes were blue, weren't they? Oh God, if I drew what I remembered of you there would be so much empty space. I suppose, though, that now you are a buried body, empty space is all you have left to be, so as much as I wish for a photograph of you to mount itself onto the wall above our bed I know that you, as I remember you, and what you are on your way to being, are much the same. Maybe we'll meet in the middle somewhere. Let's hurry. Disappear, Eleanor.

There is a shuffling sound coming from Every's room. She is awake now, too. I have to go, though I know you'll come with me in the breath I carry out of this room. Maybe if Every and I put our faces together and breathe together we can make you out of us. I hope today goes slowly. Maybe if we freeze it will help. Then we can thaw for the next three seasons until we feel you coming again.

This is an awful way to end a letter, but I am comforted by knowing that there will be more in which I can try to sound the way I want to, because I have not managed to do that here. And you will never read any of them, no one will, so only I will know this, that is, unless another person looks at me:

I miss you desperately.

3/12/_____

I miss her a lot too.

Dear Every,

I'm trying to live with what there is, not what there used to be, or worse, what there never was. You are too. You left primary school in July and you weren't worried about not seeing Katie and Rebecca anymore. You never said their names again after you said goodbye at the gates. All your missing is taken up by one person and the less there is around you the less there is to waste. At least, I suppose that's the way you see it. I'm trying to understand it and it really isn't too hard - it would be the same for me if you didn't exist. Missing her is all there is, that's one way to think of us these days.

   Big school, as you call it, doesn't seem like much to you. It worries your teachers, whose names I can't remember. There are too many of them. Apparently you're supposed to seem a lot more scared, and to be upset that you aren't making friends. They call you Eve. It's like they're talking to me about somebody else. I've corrected them but they think Every is a name likely to get you bothered by some of the other children. 'Eve should try making friends.' I suppose it bothers me that you haven't made any yet, but if you have no desire to actually cultivate friendships then why should anyone make you? Maybe one day you'll have one, but you were never closer to Katie and Rebecca than you were when you were five. You only ever grew apart. That's what growing up is. I do hope you'll grow towards someone - I hope you have already - but for now it is only yourself that you spend much time with. The 'you' you spend it with is different to the one I started writing to. She was small, and watching her was like watching everything come towards me, but the one we have now has started hiding away. Most of all I see it in your clothed body, which I haven't seen for years and would be unlikely to recognise if I saw it again without your face to label it. It strikes me now that there is no good reason for me to ever see it again. There is death, I guess. There is injury. But there is nothing good that would make me see your body once more. It's still something I wish would happen. I realise it is no longer mine, and I struggle to think of when it stopped being so. I know when I noticed it, though. I washed your clothes one day in the autumn, and there was blood in your underwear. They started later than I thought they would. I guess I never thought about it much. I always assumed you would tell me when your period started, or, to be completely honest, I assumed you would tell your mother and that she would tell me. Your silence was a brave one, but I am struck by an intuitive feeling that there was no bravery in it at all, that by not saying anything all you meant was that there was nothing much to say. You just went on with it. And even more haunting to me is that if you had said something, even now my first thought would have been to ask your mother. I say 'even now' like it's been long enough to expect that instinct to have gone away, but no, I don't think it has been that long. I don't think it ever will have been. But I am okay with that. I don't actually think it's a bad thing at all. I think it's right. She died as the person I'd have asked so since death only solidifies the past, that's the way she'll stay. Do you ever ask her questions, Every? There must be so much you never asked her. So much that I would be useless for.

I look at you now and the child in you is disappearing. But what I see, what I have, is all I want of you. My eyes are like claws clutching at whatever your body is, and I won't take my nails out until it bleeds so much that it becomes something else. And that is what it is doing, always. It's just that sometimes I don't see the blood until you've already gone. It's getting hard to keep up.

You have to understand something about life that's gone. Yours, I mean. Mine. Anyone's. There are parts of it that you do not own. You are the only person who is always with you, from beginning to end, and that is only because you have to be. We'd all choose to be somewhere else, more than we think we would, if we had the choice. A lot of people waste a lot of life trying to get away, but it doesn't work. But what I mean is that your life is not for you, and that when something seems important, it's usually because it's for somebody else. You have to let them have those parts. Now, there's a lot of my life that's for your mother, and I'll leave those parts with her, but there's a way the body has of finalising things and I need you to know that the child you've been before owns a lot of my life. I hope you take it forward with you. The times I've waited somewhere for you are yours, and so is the moment you came. And as I'm writing, right now, this part of my life is yours. It is not mine and neither is the time you are reading it, whatever I'm doing. It will not matter. There's only so much of one person's life to go around, but if you can let some of it go into someone else then suddenly there's a lot more than you thought.

Leave everything where it's meant to be, Every. Yourself, me, your mother.

I can hear you listening to your heartbeat. You of course still think it's hers.

Forgive me,
Dad

3/12/_____

No.

4/12/_____

Dear Dad,

I first saw Mum's memory box in your drawer when you asked me to get you some socks, and I've seen it since when I've just been poking around. I don't think you've hidden it from me but you've never shown it to me either. I've never thought about it much before, but sometimes I remember that between your socks and your ties, there's a little purple box with Mum's name on it. I never opened it until yesterday. You were downstairs cooking - I think it was the sound of frying - and I took my shoes off before I walked into your room in case I made a noise the crackles of the oil didn't mask. I guess I knew I shouldn't be looking. I'm sorry.

I don't know what I expected to find, but I was surprised that most of the things in there seemed like things you could keep outside of a box. There was a pinecone, an old locket with nothing in it, some bracelets, a few dinner receipts, a handful of pebbles, your anniversary cards, and the letters. I imagined the pinecone came from the park. I imagined the pebbles came from the beach. I could be wrong, I guess. The letters were folded once across the middle. The handwriting showed through the back and I thought they were from Mum to you. Somehow it seems like it would have been less intrusive of me if that's what I'd found, but when I saw that they said Dear Every, the blood at the sides of my neck pushed at the skin. I know you keep them in the box just to keep them secret, but it's weird that something meant for me is in a memory box. I don't feel like a memory.

I miss Mum. I don't think I miss her the same as you but I do miss her. I remember some of what you've written about, like the beach, and like when she died. I remember other things too. I remember her sitting with me when I tried to sleep, and I remember the three of us playing Cluedo together. I'd always just guess who it was because I never quite got how that game worked. It annoyed you and it was funny. Mostly I remember Mum trying to teach me to play the piano. I played in her lap, and she always taught me with her arm covered because I kept getting distracted by her scars. They looked kind of nice, like they were stroking her. I never really got on with the piano too well but it was nice watching her play. The tunes used to stick in my head. I'm not sure when the last one left but it's been gone a long time. I don't touch that piano anymore even though the tune is in there somewhere, at least it would be if I tried the keys long enough. You don't play it either but I don't think you ever did. It's just quiet now.

The thing is, I miss you too. Mum's been gone a while but since then and for a while before that it's felt like I've lost more than one parent. It looks like it too, the way you move like lifting your leg to walk is some great insult to someone. It might just be that Mum's not there to fill the rest of the space and maybe that highlights what is or isn't left, but you and me, when we're together, we're not that much. And I don't think I can get you back, because I can't remember what you were like before. Except for when you were annoyed at me for ruining Cluedo, but that's gone too.

I'm upset about my heart. I didn't listen to it for long last night. I sat with my laptop on the end of my bed, and the light was dimmed and blue. The last light outside my room turned off as you went to bed and then the floor creaked a few times before it went quiet. Creaks can't echo, can they? I don't know how long I sat there fiddling with the play button for. I moved my finger back and forth on the trackpad, listening to a few beats at a time. It was the first night in a long time that I went to sleep without the heartbeat playing, like the first time a baby has to sleep without a lullaby. The longer I stayed sat there, the more my reflection showed through the icons on the screen, washed out and faded like sunbleach. And then I felt my heart inside me, and I heard it through my chest or I imagined I did, and so I laid down, and no matter how I laid there, my heart kept throbbing at me like it was punching me in the chest. I have to listen to it all the time and it won't stop.

Love, I suppose,
Eve

P.S. I have a photo of Mum from a long time ago that she gave me. It's from before I was born and it's supposed to be a secret. I don't know when to show it to you. Probably when I give you this letter. Whenever that happens. I think I'll keep it like you keep your ones to me and maybe we can give them to each other at the same time. She looks really beautiful in that photo Dad. She looks a lot like me even though I don't think I look very beautiful.

Dear Eleanor,

This feels like a prayer. Like I'm talking to someone who isn't listening, and who can't. I don't know if Every talks to you too, she seems a bit too quiet to do that. I wish she would. It would be nice to listen. There have been entire days when I haven't heard her voice. Those are days when her place in my life is much the same as yours. Ghostly, even though I see her. Maybe that makes it worse, I don't know. I don't know if she can remember anything she ever said to you, and for the sake of a worthwhile memory, now is not too late to start. It would still be a memory. It would still be good enough.

Every time I look out of the kitchen window now, I see your fading name. And I stare for such a long time that when I turn away the sight still lingers in the image of anything else I look at. Even Every. I have wished heart attacks upon myself when that's happened - they sound pleasant in comparison. And then you go back to wherever it is you usually are, and there she is, lonely, I imagine, looking at me, and I know she doesn't speak because there's nothing here to speak to. All I am now is your fingerprint. That might be a bit closer than even I want you to be.

She's old enough now not to hug me. How is that something to grow out of? It does still happen, and sometimes she even kisses me goodnight. I wish I could treasure it, but the only thing I ever feel is myself preparing for the wait for it to happen again. There is nothing in between. It's a hard thing to recover from, a life the way it was. Well, you would know. But you never really did recover, did you? Will I? I shouldn't be asking you, you can never answer. I should ask Every. I should write it down and give it to her one day and then she can answer all of these questions and we can both laugh at me for ever having asked them. That would be a good day. Why I'm not asking her, I don't know.

She didn't hug me today, but she did breathe next to me, on purpose I am sure, like I've wanted her to. And there you were, for the both of us. She kissed me on the cheek and in the cold all I felt was the cold, and she didn't say anything but her lips were on my cheek for long enough that I know she was trying to make sure I would remember it. I think it was a gift. I really should thank her.

It won't be cold a lot longer, it's nearly midnight. I always put the heating back on when I go to sleep so that Every won't wake up thinking you're here again. Today has been a day of not speaking. She came home from school and I think just breathing in this place was all she wanted. It must have been horrible for her at school, knowing you were here and not for much longer. She lit her own candles in her room and she has not sat with me except for our cold candlelit dinner. I think this has become her real birthday, her own is just the start of counting down the days until the fifth.

Look, I know I never should have started this, but what a gift.

Maybe one day the cold will get so much that it will catch your ghost in ice and we'll be able to touch you again. We'll melt with you, and we look forward to it. This is the only day either of us wants anymore.

Love,
David and Every

6/12/_____

Dad I didn't write that. Don't say it's from me. I kissed you because I don't want the fifth anymore and I wish I could kiss it goodbye.

But well if it's sticking around then at least it hurts.

Dear Every,

You have come to feel so apart from me now that I barely feel like your life has anything to do with mine. We may as well be ghosts from different realms and just haunting the same space. The quietness here has got louder and louder all year and soon I fear my ears may shatter from it. It gnaws at me. If I am right, and I believe that I am because I have tested this hypothesis over and over again, you have mastered avoiding me. I have a routine. I can't help that. I have to get up and get ready and leave for work and the like, and you seem to have designed your own morning around avoiding mine. Today was the same. My alarm went off at six thirty as always, then I heard your door open and the bathroom door close. I hit snooze. That is habit. I heard the shower spraying onto the floor until the sound deadened as you stepped into it and it hit your skin instead. I waited without closing my eyes in case I fell back asleep, and then I felt it coming on heavy so I sat up instead. You are always out of the bathroom just before my alarm goes off again. I don't know how you time it so well but whatever you do, it works. The shower turned off. That was my cue. I stood and opened the door by the thinnest degree so that not even the light had an easy way through. The shower dripped every few seconds, slowing and thickening each time. About a minute before my alarm went off again, the bathroom door clicked open and the light somehow shifted and I had to blink my eyes back into seeing through it. You emerged from the bathroom and took quiet, quick steps into your room. There was a space between two of your steps where a flash of you shot through my vision. I couldn't even tell what colour the towel was. We have some that are blue, some that are white. You closed your door with a softened shut, the way you hold the handle down until the catch can slip in without a click. But not without a sound, as I have trained myself to find it. It was maybe ten seconds after your door closed that my alarm repeated. I fumbled with my phone and shut it off. The bathroom was emptying itself of steam, glowing yellow from the way the window angled the light in. I went in for my shower. I could smell you. I washed with soap, unscented.

I don't know what it is that stops me from coming out and saying Good Morning, or Happy Birthday, or even saying nothing at all and just smiling at you instead. Perhaps it is my believing that you don't want me to. Perhaps it is the fear that you will look right through me. Or perhaps it is in my knowing that there is very little here for you to look at in the first place. You see, your mother used to define my life, then the both of you did, and now she's dead and you are as absent as you can make it and I don't know what the bigger waste is: my empty body or the two wonderful lives that emptied themselves uselessly around it. I see how quiet you are, how you've learned to walk without much more than a patter, and I worry that you have become an amalgam of your mother's death and my life, two things which don't seem so paradoxical anymore. I hope that by the time you read this it's all different, but I am starting to doubt that. Whatever is left of me, whatever you are, we don't have to be damned just yet. Neither of us are your mother. Don't you be her, Every, not ever, that end writes itself too easily. Don't you bother.

After that, the day passed meaninglessly, as they have a tendency to, and I didn't see you until a few minutes ago. I was washing up. The water was a little hot and I saw my hands redden under the soap. The dishes and the glasses and the cutlery all clinked together sharply and the bubbles popped like cereal, and above me the strained floorboards ached out a yawn. A door upstairs closed. It didn't lock. Footsteps were heavy, heavier than usual, and I wondered if you were stepping that way so that I would hear you. Unlikely, I remember thinking. Strings of spit stretched in my mouth and broke off as I moved my head. I swallowed. My throat sounded mechanical. It used to be that when I got into one of these states where every sound catches me out, it would be your voice that would set me straight again. Gosh, that must be a long time gone. Now I don't hear it much, and I often have to find my own way out through the radio or by reading to myself. Not today though. No, not today. Upstairs, to the left of the floorboards and beyond the closing doors, something shattered. Everything around me fell silent. I walked upstairs with my hands still dripping water and soap. Your door was open, your room empty. There was a scratching noise coming from the bathroom. I pushed the door open. I said your name through a drying throat, and there you were, picking shards of glass up off the floor beneath the remains of a broken mirror. I said, 'Every, your feet,' because your feet were bare, and your toes were perched hard on the floor from the way you had knelt down.

'It's okay,' you said, and it froze me.

Your mother used to have this way of speaking, this voice that sunk low and grey and refrained from inflection. She spoke slowly. She would not look at me. It came from the throat, gravelly, almost a growl. And she told me several times in that voice that 'it was okay.' It meant nothing near that. It was the way her voice came out when she was done trying, when she was exhausted from the effort, when she was looking in on a part of herself that she didn't want to see. And Every, that was the exact sound you made when you told me it was okay. You startled me, I guess that's what I'm trying to say, and I backed away.

'Every.'

'I'll clean it up.'

It came out on the same damn sound. I wished I'd said nothing, because then you'd have said nothing.

'Be careful,' I said.

As soon as I spoke, I felt myself prepare to leave the words behind, in there, with you. I recall the sight of you

117

as I stepped out. You were staring straight down, the glass reflecting a hundred images back at you. I wondered what you looked like in the shards, whether you looked small, or fractured. The door shut some of the sight off from me as I pulled it to, until all I could see were your fingers beginning to fiddle with the glass. I don't know what I thought. I don't know what I felt.

The door closed when I was on the stairs. It locked when I reached the bottom.

I know that it was unsafe to leave you and I know that you are not safe while I sit here doing this, but god, forgive me, I am a coward.

3/12/_____

Dear Dad,

I have just read your letter. This year was the first time I knew a letter was coming. That knowledge has lurked in me for twelve months, and although it hasn't always been at the front of my mind, it has never gone far. It has been with me at school while my teachers asked their questions, it has been with me when the nearest people I have to friends asked if I was okay, and it has been with me when I replied, 'Yes.' Sometimes it was a lie. Not always. I wonder if I used that shuddering voice you mentioned. I do know it.

You are right. I avoid you. Yesterday morning, my alarm went off ten minutes before yours. The air was still cold from the night and the radiators were only just beginning to burn away the chill. I waited under the covers to hear your alarm from down the hall. It was a long wait. It always is - ten minutes can feel like hours. I laid there thinking about the day, and about how a birthday feels like nothing now. I must have looked forward to it at some point, mustn't I? The cold pricked at my toes, and I closed my eyes at the thought of having to use them, at the work that takes. And I'm closing them now too, at the thought of admitting that.

Why do I think that's an admission, Dad? Why do I think that?

Your alarm was so loud it seemed like it was sounding from inside my own head. It pulled at my eyes and I spun out of bed almost automatically as though routine had morphed into muscle memory. The covers came with me and I shook them away, leaving them draped between the edge of the bed and the carpet, a trail towards the door. I scuttled really, and I probably could have fallen out of the room and across the corridor. I locked the bathroom door and let my towel drop into a heap beside the toilet. The shower was warm, always set to thirty eight, and I washed as it reached temperature and the steam began to fill the room. I stared at the wall that was inches from my face and I could see a faint reflection of myself on the tile, disappearing ever so slowly as the steam started to cobweb to the surface. I looked harder, but I was gone. I turned the temperature up, slowly. The shower took a moment to warm up and then the warming started turning my skin pink. I held onto the tap and I turned it again. My shoulder flinched and my back wormed away under the water. I breathed in sharply a few times before the heat finally took over the pool around my feet.

One more twist of the tap.

I stood there with my eyes scrunched, twisting my neck into the stream. The heat turned up a lot sooner that time, and the burning on my skin felt like a claw, gripping at my neck, scratching down my spine, running its fingers down all of me. I lasted maybe ten seconds in there. Not far off my best.

I caught my breath - it's funny how that takes it out of you. Skin cooling is a peculiar sensation. It happens almost immediately, but the afterburn is a real stickler.

I set the shower back to thirty eight. For you.

I stood outside the shower on the mat, which felt neither hot nor cold, neither a friend nor antagonist, and that was a welcome ambiguity. The room was a blur through the steam. It had clung to everything. Walls, pipes, a watchface left by the soapdish. It had gone for the glass first, of course. The shower door and then the window, although it was hard to tell the steam from the patterns in the glass. I didn't see the mirror mist up, but I have watched it enough to know that it happened slowly. Still I looked into it, harder than I did into the tile, and I carried on looking at nothing, and it carried on concealing something, and I remembered, gradually, what you said once about Mum and me staring into it together. Something about sharing, us and not you. You said you wanted to see the mirror broken one day.

That evening I'd been home two hours, maybe three, and I still hadn't seen you. I know I make it that way, but from your letter it sounds like you're part of that effort too. I thought you looked through your door at me and, now that I know, I am glad that you do. Maybe I should walk slower. I was fiddling with my phone at my desk. I heard you moving around downstairs, then I heard you moving around less, then I didn't hear you much at all. You sounded as gone as you think I am. I set the phone down. I sat as still and as silent as I could, with my jacket taken off and hanging on the chair, because if I wore it, it rustled when I breathed. That's something I wish I could do just a little bit less. I don't need it to stop, but I imagine breathing less would make everything pass a little slower. I sat, listening to the sound of your absence, and to the insistence of my heart for me to hear it, and to the rising hoarseness of my breathing. Even quiet breath deafens when it's all there is. The breath turned into a wince, and the wince to a sob, and the sob into looming tears, at which I quivered and sighed to turn them back into me. It worked, more or less. The walk to the bathroom wasn't my quietest, as you know.

I always thought that people closed the door behind them when they were sad, and that they leaned their back against it. That they lifted their chin to look up. Their eyes shut tight but tears get through anyway, and they groan with frustration at the loss of control. It turned out that's not what happens, at least not when it's me. I closed the door (that part's the same, for what it's worth) and it was just really depressingly quiet in there too. Jesus.

I walked to where the mirror was and watched my reflection warp in the tap underneath it. I turned my head and the reflection turned tighter, and reflections from the tiles and handles and the mirror worked their way in too. The mirror grew in the chrome as I played with where my head was. Then it settled when I did, and it took over the entire reflection. I looked up. I looked at the mirror. I hit the damn thing. The picture in the tap shook and shone. The mirror didn't break so I punched it again, and again it didn't break so I punched it twice, then it cracked and I kept hitting it until it smashed. I don't know if it was a really strong mirror or if I'm just a really bad puncher. I had imagined it breaking into hundreds of pieces like rainfall, but it came out in a few large shards that only shattered properly when they hit the sink and the floor. My knuckles were red but they weren't cut. I was surprised by that. I tried not to move my feet too much as the glass had gone everywhere, but I had to turn a little. I heard the glass crunch under me. I didn't hear it cut me. Then I heard your footsteps. I didn't hear your voice.

I thought that you would be calling for me. I had left the door unlocked and I thought you would come flying in, exasperated, needing to know what had happened. I thought you would see that my hand was red and getting redder, and I was certain you would dive straight to the floor and check me all over, tearing your feet on the glass and not caring, and getting me out of the bathroom as near to unscathed as you could. But you didn't. The door nudged open politely as though it was an intrusion. I could make out the shape of you even with one eye on the glass, and you moved hardly at all, let alone rushed to help me. You said some useless words. That low voice came out of me. And you were gone again, so I locked you out. I know from your letter that you were worried when you left, but you needn't be. Nothing happened.

Nothing happened at all. Well, maybe not nothing - I cried. And I wished you'd come back.

Love from Eve x

Dear Eleanor,

I have taken the day off work. I think that's what I will do every year on the fifth. Every is at school, or she will be in a few minutes, and in the same breath that she walked out of the front door, I picked up my pen. It was a long breath, that one. I made it last. I opened your memory box and put all the other letters in front of me, folded so I couldn't read them, and took out this year's blank paper. And now I'm going to write, that's all I'm going to do. I'm going to sit at my desk and draw out these words and I won't stop, I promise you this, until Every gets home, which she usually does between three forty two and three fifty. I expect it will be sooner today, because this is the only place she wants to be. This is the only day of the year that happens and it's something we have to savour.

I made Every breakfast today. I'm afraid I can't say that happens enough, but I can't say she's there to eat it very often either. She likes mushrooms on toast, same as me. I used to make it every morning until it went cold most mornings, and now I only make it on the occasion I know she will want it. I made it early, while the dark outside was still heavy, and I cooked it with the back door open so that it wouldn't get too hot inside. It is the cold, after all, that we see you in. She came downstairs very early. 'Have you been awake long?' I asked.

'Mm.'

125

'There's food.'

'Thanks.'

It was amongst the longest conversations we'd had of late. Every ate, and I watched her. She gazed through the door at a faint shape in the dark, her elbows pulled tight to her body, leaning into her plate. She still struggles with the cold. I stood there, sleeves rolled up, trembles tracing my arms. Each time she swallowed, a waft of breath escaped. She looked into every one of them.

'Will you be okay today?' she asked me, without looking up.

I went to say Yes, but my mouth wouldn't form it, so I nodded. She wasn't watching, so I laboured with the word until it came out, or mostly it did. She nodded once, the way the elderly acknowledge shame. Her fork was in one of the last slices of mushroom, and she fiddled with it between each of her fingers. The fork clinked against the plate and screeched when it dragged. 'Will you be?' I asked.

'Mm.'

I was glad it wasn't the sort of answer you can respond to. She did not finish her breakfast, but at least she had eaten something.

'Why do I have to go to school today?'

'You have to go to school.'

'You don't have to go to work.'

'You have to go to school.'

Seconds passed, then I removed her plate as she stood.

'Okay,' she said.

Before she left, she put her hand on my arm and said, 'Bye, Dad,' in a whisper so slight it was hardly a voice, and she watched her breath find my face. We both did. She disappeared down the corridor, then her footsteps faded into it, then she closed the door behind her and shut me in with you, in these mists you cast over our whole house, and my life was a perfect one for the first time since… I don't know, some time in the past. Every gave me that moment. I really thought there might never be another one. But there you go. There it is. I've learned enough about these moments to know that I can't slow them down enough because they go as soon as they come, so I am breathing very softly. Every brush of breath in front of me paints the air carefully, and I know that, for now, you are taking care of me. I'm going to write all the way through. Then I'm going to spend the evening with my daughter. She is my solace.

I have a glass of water. I will sip it very slowly because I want to leave the table as little as possible. If my hand freezes then I'll trust my heart to shiver the words out of the pen, for that is where they come from. I don't even care what I write, because whatever it is, it is for you. It is a devotion.

It is nine twenty two. Every is at school. I have hours with you. Writing will keep me with you, and the slower I can do it the better. I know it won't make the time last any longer but I'll be grateful for the illusion.

I spent a minute on 'illusion' and what a minute it was.

What should I tell you? What do you want to know? It would help if I knew how much you know already, how much you see. Is it only today you are with us or do you watch from a distance all year long? I'll never know, and spending hours trying is beginning to seem like a pointless way to spend time. God, there's been so much time passed like that. So much of it gone to things that never were and never will be. I guess they were never 'things' to begin with. Things - William Carlos Williams, right? You liked him so much! Oh good lord, this is the flurry of lost memories coming back to see me! I thought they'd gone.

I'm remembering when you first read Williams to me. You read his poem, that one about plums in the fridge, and you loved that poem like a person, I'm sure of it. You had that look on your face, the same one I hope you would have on it if you could read this, and it's the same one I hope Every will have when she reads my letters to her. I remember I copied the poem out, stuck it on the fridge, and left plums in it for you. You never said anything about it to me, and when I came home to you like it had never happened, but knowing it had, it was the most wonderful feeling. The most wonderful one then anyway. Well, every feeling is the most wonderful feeling at that moment it comes, isn't it?

This is the most wonderful feeling.

I just want to sit here. I want my pen to touch the paper and not move unless I can move it without meaning to (now *there* would be an honest word) and just sit frozen in the same cold you are present in and wait for more memories to come back like that one did, ones that used to be pointless to remember but seem to have found their place in me.

It is almost eleven o'clock and I have been sitting here for minutes. Nothing new has come to me but my pen hasn't left the paper. My hand hurts but, well, you know what I think of that. I've only just realised how quiet it is. My mind has been running so fast that the blood at my eardrums has been music to me, and I've been listening, and I've been lost. But as soon as you notice something like that you can't listen anymore, and it's gone because it's in the secrecy, in the shadows, that it lived.

That reminds me. I remember when you told me about the scars on your stomach.

It was one of our early dates, and it must have been winter because it was dark and it was still early. We had been out for dinner. I can't remember what food it was or what it was like, but afterwards we stood near a bus stop. We fumbled our way around saying goodnight and not wanting to. We were a couple of arms lengths away from each other. My arm kept drifting towards you, imperceptibly, at least to you. I remember the glow of the orange lamplight on your face, and I remember squinting slightly from the headlights of the passing cars shining into mine. I think the drizzle got into them too.

'I can walk from here,' you said.

You looked in the direction of home. It was down a couple of alleyways, but then that never did bother you.

'Yeah, I'm that way.' I pointed limply in the opposite direction.

We held eye contact for long enough that if we were a movie we would have had to kiss passionately with some tremendous orchestra crescendo accompanying us.

'I should tell you something,' you said.

'Okay,' I said, breaking the eye contact out of worry at goodness knows what. I guess I must have thought you'd had enough of me.

'You know my arm. The cuts on it.'

I looked back up.

'I've got them all over my stomach.'

I wanted to ask what had happened to you, I wanted to tell you there was nothing to worry about anymore, I wanted to tell you I wasn't scared, that I was ready for this, and that I knew exactly what to do.

I said, 'Okay.' I suppose it was a start.

'I'll see you soon,' you said.

'Yeah.'

You walked home. I watched you go, disappearing into the darkness long before you made it to the alleyway. And I stood there a while, and I thought about what you had said, and I tried not to think that I didn't know what to do, but that was the truth, and I thought it eventually, a few times over, until it was the only thought left. I stood there a little longer and the evening started to pass me by, the way it always does. I let it, the way I always do.

I have been doing that again, if, in fact, I ever stopped. Every was in some trouble the other day, I think. She broke the mirror, and I went up to see what had happened. She was knelt amongst the glass and she told me she was fine, but it was so unconvincing that it was practically a warning. She said she was clearing it up, and I left her - I tried to let it pass. She locked the door behind me with a sound so deep she may as well have been locking herself into an endless chamber. I walked away, and I walked away slowly. No sound came from the bathroom. If she had been clearing it up surely there would have been some noise? Goodness knows what she was doing, but I don't need to know to be overcome with insistent imagination. The way I am forced to think of it, she chose a piece of glass from the floor like a piece of fruit from a tree. She looked for a piece big enough to grip, with an edge sharp enough to cut without trying. She stood up, feet scratching against the glass, and sat on the toilet. I guess she stared at the glass for a while, looking at every edge and trying out the different ways of holding it. She rolled her sleeve up to her elbow. She held the glass very close to her skin, maybe at an armhair's distance, and then she touched it to her skin lightly. The skin depressed and she let go. A red mark slowly appeared. She pushed into it again, harder this time, then let it go. Either the glass or the skin made a light snapping sound as she let it go again. She picked her spot elsewhere, nearer the wrist this time than the elbow. She touched the glass to her skin across that thin bone beneath the base of her thumb. She pushed, then she changed her mind, and she moved it off the bone. She went back to the middle where there was some meat to get into. She pushed the glass against the skin as hard as she could make herself push. She closed her eyes. She tightened her hand around the glass, trying to pull but not quite wanting to. She let out a faint whimper. She wondered if pushing the glass had been enough alone to break the skin, but she didn't want to lift it away to check. She felt the muscles all the way up her arm tighten, ready to make the cut, and she rehearsed the motion in her mind. She'd been holding the glass there for nearly a minute when every thought in her head finally fell away, and she sliced the glass across her wrist. She grimaced. She didn't make much of a sound, but she let the blood out like a swimmer coming up for air. I guess that was the point. She looked, and there was blood. She put the glass down, carefully. She watched the blood start to run down her arm, turning cold almost as soon as it met the air. The trail dried.

When I went back to the bathroom she had cleaned everything up, and she had done a damn fine job of it too. I should get her to clean the bathroom more often. I looked for any sign of what she had done, any stray speck of blood or some forgotten, bloodied tissue. There was none. She'd been very meticulous. She was in her room by that point, and I did not see her again that day. I sat downstairs with my scarless arms. I sat downstairs with my tearstained face. Our separate sadnesses had got us. They are quite something to endure. Mine is anyway. Hers must, god, hers must be. You know, I've never really thought too much until recently what it must be like for her. I think that was a conscious decision, shamefully. That poor girl.

She will not be without you much longer today. The candles are lit and the door is open so the candleflames are swaying. I could get up close to one and it would still be cold enough in here to feel you.

No. I'll hold my pen against the paper, press very, very hard, and wait for the next two hours and fifty something minutes to give me my daughter back. She is my solace.

I'm looking ahead of me as I write this: I'll wait.

6/12/_____

Oh no, Dad.

Dear Every,

The woman you're going to be is starting to shape herself in you. There are mannerisms of yours, and flinches, that have been so stubborn that now they'll stay there forever. I have some of my own, like the odd need to stretch my eyelids. I've been doing that since I was somethingteen and I gave up getting rid of it a long time ago. Now I just make sure that when I do it, no one's looking me in the eyes. Saves me the embarrassment. Then again, people making eye contact with me is quite rare these days, as is people making any real contact with me at all. I'm not sure how that happened. Lucky me. Stretch away.

Your flinches are more subtle, and you're at the age when the rest of your body is still learning itself, so while for me stretching my eyes is all I can think of, for you it's more like your walk is now of your own inescapable kind, and your face has found a number of ways to combat that rare smile of yours when it finally does show up.

I have watched from a distance of late, but at least I have watched. All of last winter, and this winter too, you have spent a lot less time in your room and a lot more of it in the garden. Our garden has not been kept well these last few years. It never was my strong point. I manage to cut the grass here and there, and trim the edges, but I find myself glad of our decision when you were small to lay a path from the back door to the bottom of the garden with stones. It keeps things a little simpler out there. As soon as the temperature started to fall this year, around October, you put your boots on and went a few steps outside, breathing out heavy and long. To anyone else it would have looked like a game, but you were fixated on the inches ahead of your face, looking for the air to freeze your breath and for it to swirl in front of you the way our breath does on the fifth. It did not happen in October, so you did not stay out for long. There was the odd hour that was cold enough early after sunrise on a few November mornings, and you moved your boots to the back door in anticipation of them. You put them on and stood out there, and when I stared out through the window and you caught me watching, you were not quick to look away. You were not quick to do anything, and what breath there was for you out there fell out of your mouth like spit. It did not clear quickly. Those were heavy dawns.

The most recent of those mornings was three, maybe four, days ago, and it lingered a little longer. Your boots were gone from the doormat by the time I got up, and the door was open a little, so I put on my coat to watch you. You kicked lightly at the frosted grass, and following each kick you let out a breath, thicker than on other mornings, fading to mist in time for the next. I recognised that kick, loose at the ankle, as exactly how your mother would stand when she was nervous. That wasn't very often. Hers was such a slow-moving existence that she was braced for anything long before it came. No, that is nonsense, it must be, and I mustn't romanticise. I wonder, now that I think of it, how often I read her wrong. How often I still do in retrospect. And how often I do the same to you.

Either way, you kicked at the grass and scratched into the soil, with your eyes on the ground so fixatedly that I don't think you saw me. I backed away to the table. I could not see you from there. Over my toast, I thought with great effort about how I felt, and the feelings fought back with such ferocity that I could not tell one side from the other, and they were determined not to let me. I remember having a hand hugged around my tea, gripped like an anchor. I remember thinking that my skin was tougher than it used to be, though I could not really tell from looking. I suppose I should be pleased, pleased that you have found another way to keep your mother with you when she was really all you wanted, and I suppose I should be worried that nothing has come close to making you feel otherwise, and I suppose I should be regretful that I have allowed both of those to happen, and perhaps that is how I feel, but as is often the case with emotion, I would rather just stare at my hand clutching at the cup. That I can understand.

I was surprised at how clear it was when I said Good Morning to you. It felt thin, and wavering. You responded as though it wasn't. That's good. I had left you some toast under the grill and it was just about warm enough to eat. You ate hunched over, eyes hidden in your hair, and the toast must have been more crisp than it seemed because it was loud when you chewed. Then it quietened. God, it quietened.

There's this incredible little twitch in your right eye. I watched it closely. The side nearest your ear shrinks quite quickly, like its own little heart that doesn't need to beat that often. I've no idea why I like watching it so much. I've even tried to take it on myself so I could take a little bit of you with me wherever I go (most people would put a photograph in their wallet, but well...) but I think it's something that either comes by itself or it doesn't. And there's this beautiful movement your mouth makes. Again it's just the corner, and it lifts up a snap. It looks like your smile is on its way but it goes away as fast as it came. The tease is excruciating. They're just little explosions, and the cavities are all in me. Some things don't change.

You know when you stare at something so long that you completely miss when it changes? Well, when I snapped out of it you were taking my plate away, and then I let the mug go too. I've no idea if the tea had gone cold, and I've no idea if I drank it. You washed up with your back mostly to me, which was not on purpose unless you only chose to wash up because you knew it would mean your back was turned. I doubt it. I watched anyway, and I watched for a tremor or a twitch. But you did me one better - I think I caught a smile. They do happen! I'll admit it was only the slightest version of it, without teeth or accompanying sound, but I remember it vividly, under the shadows of your face, or so perhaps you thought. I'm always looking, love, you can't hide it! You were looking down at the plates, and all of a sudden your face lifted so slightly, and you stopped moving for a split second, and there it was, a ghost of itself but a ghost of the flesh, the same smile your mother and I used to admire together as the most important thing ever to happen to a world. I'm sure the world would disagree if it knew, but since when did we mind what the world thinks of us?

I wonder what thought it was that brought that smile on. An unconscious one, I hope. One you never knew the content of but knew afterwards had happened, and you knew it was worth having, and worth feeling and forgetting, and your face had no choice but to smile at whatever the thought had been. Or maybe it was a conscious thought, something deliberate and small. Perhaps it was something you had seen outside. I suppose you'll have already forgotten it happened, maybe you never even noticed that it did, but I'd like to know how that smile came to be with us again. It was something I can't do for you, I know that much, because nothing I've done in a long time has made you smile, even just politely. I'd just like to know how it came about, that's all. How any of them did. They're all so important, I'll take whatever I can get.

Love,
Dad

3/12/_____

Dear Dad,

This morning wasn't cold enough to make any use of going outside. I've left my boots by the door and I'm wearing socks thick enough to keep my feet from catching a chill, because it is colder inside than out. Still not cold enough to freeze breath, not that I can tell, but I don't think there is much further to go before we get there. I know the smile you're talking about, and I know how it got there better than you think I do.

How long had I been outside for? Maybe an hour? Maybe a little over that? It's hard to keep track of time when everything you do takes up so little of it. I don't remember kicking into the dirt, and I'm sorry if that's made another job for you to do. I walk so slowly out there that I can feel the pressure as it shifts from each part of my foot, and I can feel how a toe can crackle under a body's weight. I don't even weigh that much. I breathe out slowly and softer than it seems to you, as the stream can last longer that way and there's more of a chance of me getting the fifth nearer to you. I don't know why you wait a year between it happening if it means as much as it sounds. I don't know why you wait at all. I don't breathe that way for me.

Skin warms slowly, as least it did the other day. Slower than the air did at least. I had been playing with my breath for so long I'd forgotten to notice how my fingers had numbed. It was only as the air warmed up and the breath in front of my face paled and grew more brief that I noticed the feeling in my fingers had gone. I held them up and they looked no different. I get the impression that's not the same for emotion that vanishes. That somehow shows. I haven't seen it on you, not by a long way.

I started rubbing my fingers together as I headed inside. The numbing turned to tingling and the tingling stayed as I removed my boots, and it stayed when I saw you at the table, and it stayed when you said Hello to me, and you are right, it didn't sound strange. You looked more frozen than I felt, the pale blue of your cuffs blending into the veins on the back of your hand, flesh fading against the teacup.

I didn't know how much you were watching me, and I didn't know there was that much in my face. I thought it was just a face. Narrow eyes and hair swept back over the ears. That's all. It's strange to think of how much happens on it that I don't know about, and it's strange to think of when that started. Who knows. Who needs to.

I was washing up after a quick, quiet breakfast, and I wasn't thinking of having my back turned, or of concealing anything at all. If anything, I thought of how little difference hiding would make to how either of us moves through a day. We're either barely there or we're right in front of each other, and the experience doesn't differ all that much between the two. I guess I feel like spending time outside, playing with breath like it was snow, is something I do right in front of you, but with your letters as the exception, you have never said anything about it to me. And I think about how if I had never found your letters, it would be another four years before I had even the little I have from them so far. I would not know how you think of me, or even that you think of me at all, because without your letters as context, I worry that that's what it would look like. Just a lonely man sat in the kitchen, cup in hand.

I don't see much in frozen breath, not really, but it's nice to pretend for a moment that it's the fifth, and that to your mind, Mum is here. And I trick myself into seeing her in the cloud, just a nose or her glasses, or a movement so small it seems intricate. She knew a lot about intricate movements, like all the cuts I used to see on her arms when she played piano for me. I imagine cutting them in was like painting. When I was washing up, I imagined a mist of breath showing me the picture of Mum's arm. Scars all up it, some faded, some raised. Mine's next. There was a knife in the bottom of the sink, and I ran my fingers along the edges of the handle and of the blade. It started lightly, perhaps even with water between skin and the knife at times, and I found myself going back to the blade and pushing. I pressed my finger against it about as far you can go before it scratches in. And I was surprised by how little hesitation I had as I pushed it harder into my fingertip, and pulled it across so that it cut into me. I couldn't see it or hear it, but dishsoap in an open wound stings pretty quickly. I held my finger in there. A diluted, fading bloodcloud appeared and went away. And that is when I smiled. I smiled because it's so simple, a little cut no one knows about, but it clears a mind for a moment or two, and that is better than nothing.

I've been doing that a lot Dad, actually.

Love from Eve x

Dear Eleanor,

Today should have been the day that makes all the other days worth enduring, but it hasn't been. I woke up early to light the candles downstairs and play the heartbeat for us to listen to over a quiet breakfast, but when I came in from the kitchen there was smoke coming off the candlewick and nothing else. The light was turned on. The radiators were crackling like waking bones and Every was stood in front of me and she said, in a voice too close to yours, 'It was too cold.' I froze as though it still was.

'Every, it's supposed to be,' I said. Always taking the chance to say her name. I still love it as much as ever.

She held her breath until the words couldn't stay in any longer. 'I know.' She doesn't lie to me, you see. I love that about her. It's one of those traits you don't find in many people. You'd be so happy to know it. But those words, honest as they were, came out in your voice. How many times can my feeble heart break? Can you look back and count them now that it can't happen to you anymore? Do you think there are many left for me? What about her? Please let there be less for her. I'll take them. Give them to me.

I told her we couldn't have the radiators on today, and I noticed that the air coming out with the words was invisible. Nothing. 'It'll get colder then it'll come,' I told her. She knew what I was looking for. She didn't respond, and in her silence I noticed that the heartbeat was not playing. I went around the house turning the radiators off, screwing them as tight as I could so that Every wouldn't be able to turn them up again if she tried, and when I got to her room, it was silent in there too. No heartbeat. I went back downstairs, rubbing my temples with my fingers. I moved my hand away when I got back to the living room, and I readied myself to say something, goodness knows what, but I looked up and Every wasn't there. I looked around me, and I checked in the next room, and I looked in the kitchen but she was not there either. The doormat where her boots lived was bare, and the door to the garden was swaying a little, trying to click shut. There she was outside, sheltered beneath the pear tree, and I could not understand why if she was out there with you that she couldn't just come inside with you instead. I just couldn't understand the difference. Well, then again, if there's no difference, then I don't understand why I care so much. I don't understand it at all.

I stood by the kettle, and I resisted the temptation to turn it on because that would certainly have warmed things up too much. I watched Every through the window, moving slowly, monastically, and I watched her exhale air that she watched like a movie. I lit the candles in the kitchen, and I found myself thinking about how wretched tradition is, at least this one, and how the weight of tradition holds us all too far back, when maybe we should just get on with giving up, because that's all this is starting to look like.

As I watched her through the window, dust and light came together to illuminate where Every had traced your name in the glass. I hadn't washed it once. Every spotted me, and she drifted towards me. It took a while longer than it needed to, which I think should probably be our motto. She stood on the other side of the glass, shoulders hunched up to her neck. I breathed onto your name, and I traced my finger over it. Every did too, although from that side her breath didn't do that much. I watched her. She stared only at your name. And it was as it faded, as my fingernail traced your name again, that Every struck the glass with her palm. It jolted me. I hopped backwards and only just missed a candle. She struck it again. The thud muted my telling her not to. I stood back, fingertips dancing in palms. The glass cracked once across the middle on the third strike and then she took a fist to it, and a couple of punches later, it shattered. It fell and there was quiet. She breathed through an open mouth, blood right under the surface of her cheeks and forehead. Somehow the glass didn't cut her.

Your name has been scattered across the kitchen floor all afternoon. We'll be catching ourselves on it for days. Every did not stick around for long, and she has not been back yet even though it has been dark an hour or two now. I have sat here with the house silent and its deceased in shards around me. I expect I will be asleep before

Every gets home. She's left it as cold in here as it is outside.

Take today. I don't want it.

And I don't want another one.

6/12/_____

I already took it.

Dear Every,

Last December we had a white Christmas. It has stayed
with me all year. I don't think I've written much about our
Christmases. It's just that so much happens at the start of
December that by the end of it we've got nothing left but
loss. I suppose the only exceptions are the Christmases
when your mother was still here, and last year's. There
can't be any way you'll remember those early ones, so let
me think.

Our first one. You were three weeks old. You didn't
know what was going on, or that anything was going on
at all, which was good news for us because we didn't
know what the hell we were doing. There were no
grandparents to come and relive their old Christmases
through you, no parents in the family to come and tell us
what to do, and no family really at all. We had some
friends. They had children. They were having their own
Christmases and they left us to it, for which I am grateful
because we didn't want anyone else anyway, but they had
told us about that wonderful first Christmas: there isn't a
lot to it. They weren't around after it. No one really stays
here if they don't have to, and we didn't stay in touch.
That could be the thing I'm just about the worst at, as you
can probably tell by my proclivity for writing letters and
not sending them! That Christmas was both my favourite
and your mother's. You were supposed to be born a little

later in December, and we didn't think it likely we'd have the energy to even notice Christmas, but we realised in those three weeks that all Christmas was that year was the one where we finally got the same, best gift. We bought nothing for each other. We didn't need to. And we didn't get you anything either. That was mostly my idea. Your mother wanted you to have something to remember, or I guess I should say to discover, your first Christmas by, but because of my avoidance of mementos, I kind of talked her into leaving that Christmas Day with that December twenty fifth. I don't regret that too much, I don't think.

We kept a vigil for Christmas with our sleeplessness on Christmas Eve. It was composed of as much excitement as the ones we used to lay awake through as children. What an incredible thing, to live them again with each other. You were asleep at the foot of our bed, so that any time we awoke in the night you would be right there in front of us, and you didn't wake once or make a single sound. That would be the staple of your infancy, and it would go on to worry us to no end, but for that night, before we knew anything about your life, it was wonderful just watching you silently, fireworks going off inside each of us, and us not saying a thing so we could leave your sleep uninterrupted. In the morning, just before light and before either of us yawned, you made a sound that was so near a laugh that it made us laugh with you. What a way to wake up! To laughter! Your own! We just left you to it,

x

150

and we wished each other Merry Christmas, and then we got up and each said, 'Merry Christmas, Every,' and we took you downstairs to a quiet, warm house and a slow breakfast, and a peaceful day spent beside a sparsely decorated tree. We didn't do anything. We were just there with each other. There's really nothing to say beyond that, other than that your first Christmas meal was baby formula. There's a memento, a memory, even if it's just mine.

I do wonder sometimes if I made a mistake not having photographs. I don't even think it's important to me, it's just something I do. I always wanted it to mean that I would remember my life for its effect on me (there's me talking like my life and myself are two different things!) rather than one frozen snapshot of a moment that stood out to someone. But I do wish, at times, that I had a picture of us beside that tree. It was the best way I have ever spent Christmas, and I suspect it always will be. I want to know what that happiness looked like on us, because it did not last, and I don't know how many more times I ever saw it on all three of us together. But then the fact that I pang for it so badly is perhaps the best reason to think I made the right choice, because knowing it will never come back, even in a silly photograph, means that I will always adore it for the one day it was. I do wish I had a photo of her, though, that's become a constant wish, one of her outside any time I recognise just so I could discover her face again. Maybe it was nothing like yours after all. I just want to see it, that beautiful thing, so I can remember her as something more than a stickwoman. And I want to feel it break my heart into smaller pieces than anything that has ever existed because each little break - they would happen one by one - would feel even more wonderful than the last. And as long as I never look away, my life would be perfect again. Well, as long as you were looking with me, and holding my hand, and happy. There would be nothing wonderful about it if you weren't happy.

Without a photo I see her in places I wouldn't if I had one. I think my mind is trying to make photos as I go. A couple of weeks back, I was out near the old college. I remember having dreams that you would go there, not because it's particularly good but just because I never went, and I thought that it would be momentous. It's not there anymore, and it hasn't been for a decade now. They've done nothing with the building yet and I don't suppose they will. There have been a few times it's pretended it will go on to be something - once it was luxury apartments, once a retirement village, even a spa if memory serves - but I expect it will just be empty, and then it will crumble. The building is on the way into town and I was heading in to get some bits together for Christmas. I was walking by on the other side of the road from where people still use the old parking spaces, and a couple of cars back, someone was getting out. It was a woman, and she was short, but there was something in the way that her hair didn't move much in the breeze that made my steps quicken, and that made me cross the road without looking. I don't even remember much about your mother's hair, but I suppose I don't need to, because memory has placed traps all over town and I keep falling into them. I aimed myself at the woman's car, but it was busy out, and by the time I got there she had gone. It didn't stop a faint disappointment rising, and it didn't stop me looking through the car window for your mother's things. There was a coffee cup from the same place she got hers, but well, your mother didn't even drive.

I said already that last Christmas was a white one - the only white one, actually, of your entire life so far. There might be a few more the way these winters are going. I saw your mother in Christmas too, in you again I'm sorry to say, but you didn't mean for me to see. I'll explain. Grief has this way of making kaleidoscopes, you see.

When I say it was white, I mean it in the scarcest sense. The ground was covered in frost, not snow, so thinly that footsteps burned through it in the moments before they even touched it. So there was no snowman to be built, no sledding, just the thinnest frost I had ever seen acting as a ghost of the Christmas ideal and covering the ground like misted up film. We walked on it, ruined it, separately in the garden. You were walking in circles and I was pretending to tend to the garden. We still hadn't recovered from what happened on the fifth and around it. We still haven't, I don't think, not really. But then our definition of 'recovered' is probably a bit more austere than others, so who knows how far along we are. I haven't recovered yet, I can say that much. And I don't know what that means for three days from now. But last year we melted the ground. Every one of our footsteps did. It's not the isolation I remember so much, or how slowly we moved. It was the colour you left behind when you went back inside for the afternoon. Red.

The school had been on the phone not too long before, maybe a month or thereabouts. I remember it ringing as much as I remember the conversation. It rings so seldom. A woman's voice asked if it was me, then said who she was. It was one of your teachers. 'I hope you don't mind me calling,' she said. 'I wanted to talk to you about Every.'

Well what else would she be phoning me for?

'Okay.'

'We've noticed some behaviours that we're getting a bit concerned about.'

'Oh really? Like what?'

'Well she's quite withdrawn,' she said.

Not a lot peculiar about that, I thought.

'And she's been very sullen. Have you noticed any changes in her behaviour at home?'

'No, I don't think so. I mean, she spends a lot of time in her room but most teenagers do.'

There was a pause on the line.

'Does she seem okay to you?'

'Um, I'm not sure what you mean.'

'Well, we're worried about her. We wanted to see if you were too.'

'Oh. Well not really. A little maybe. It's hard to tell to be honest, with everything she's been through.'

'Yes. Look, one of Every's teachers noticed some blood on a tissue in her pencil case.'

'What was it doing in her pencil case?' That probably wasn't the right response, but I'd imagine it gives you a tickle. Luckily for me the teacher ignored it.

'The blood was in straight lines. We often see that with young people who cut themselves.'

'I see,' I said.

She gave me a moment. I didn't really need it. It wasn't like I hadn't had the thought before. 'Do you know if that's what she's doing?'

I didn't know how to answer, which felt like it said enough. 'I'm not sure,' I said. It was near enough the truth.

'You might want to talk to her about it,' she said.

Not much chance of that, I thought.

'But it's important not to overreact.'

Not much chance of that either. She said they were there if we needed anything, and I probably said Thank You.

That phone call has played back in my head over the last few months, and it played back to me in the garden at Christmas. You walked away from me to go back inside, and I watched as you knew I would, and although your hands were in front of you, frozen as though in prayer, something fell. It was blood let calmly. There wasn't much, and I don't know if you noticed you were bleeding, but you might have, and if you did then perhaps you left it there for me. You walked up the step and disappeared inside the house, and I followed and saw just a few little drops of blood like they were from the broken leg of a crow. It sat there on the white, and I watched it, and the remains of its warmth burned through the tiny patch of frost and burned into the ground like a tear on tissue. I realised just then that I hadn't seen your arms in so long. It was not the merriest of Christmases, but then most of them never are.

The thought of sneaking into your bedroom while you're sleeping to get a quick look at your arm has been with me all year, but you don't need to worry, that won't go beyond a thought, and it's a regrettable one at that. You're older than you used to be, and wherever your privacy came from, it is something I promise to value as much as anything.

I've noticed the clothes you wear. They are never white around your arms and they always have long sleeves. Tight wristbands and thumbholes, all these little oddities to keep your arms away from me, the same ones your mother used, even after she met me. Maybe you'll tell me about it one day, because as much as I want to help it's not something I can bring myself to force on you. Is that respect or a failing? You tell me. Well it's fear, but I guess fear could be in either.

I don't want to jump to conclusions about it. I don't want to assume it's a way of bringing your mother closer to you - I'm not quite sure if you know she did it too - but I do believe there's a tendency towards this kind of behaviour that you've somehow got from her. I must say I never understood it, not really, when she explained it to me. She always spoke of it like an art she had mastered, like all the torment she held within herself was kept in some ethereal, unseen shape that she knew every part of. Containing it, making sure no one ever saw it, was what made that art so convincing. She told me that she cut herself before she got on the plane back from Michigan, and again before she got on the train home. She was bleeding when she walked in through the door, but both of her parents looked at her as though having her back was enough of a resolution. She said Hi to them both, and smiled, like she had just popped out for milk. She told me that was when the hardness in her was at its worst, but that it was also when it was okay to have it, because no one knew it was there. Apparently the blood just felt wet against her sleeve, and that was all. Pain you share only with yourself is a special kind, Every, but I don't know how much of it I've experienced. I guess that's a good thing. But it is one that, when she spoke about it, gave her the kind of solace and peace that most of us struggle to find. The look on her face when she told me about it was the look of someone missing a friend, or a lover. And I was right there. I was not enough. I never was.

It's just a bad thing to do to yourself, that's as far as my understanding of it has ever gone. Tell me what it's like, Every. Are you really that fucking sad? Am I really so far away that you'd rather reach for a razorblade?

Is it me? That's my real question. That's probably, if I'm honest, why I haven't grabbed you by the arm and pulled your damn sleeves up, because I'm scared that what I'd see is what I've done to you. Every, I'm still here. Cut me up all you want, just don't do it to yourself.

Do you even know I'm here, Every? Am I gone?

Are you?

That's jealousy. I want to know these sacred things only you and your mother know even though one of you is dead. I've tried to know them. I've even had that pathetic cinematic moment of standing in front of a mirror, looking at my waste of a self holding a razor to his wrist, and quivering around trying to touch it to his skin. I couldn't. I don't even know how you hold those things without cutting your fingers. I dropped it into the sink and it clinked so sharply. I scooped it out with one finger against the porcelain. It scratched on its way up. It sounded like someone scraping bone. I caught it in my palm when it went over the lip and I tipped it straight into the bin. I rolled my sleeves back down. Not that it made much difference. Isn't that such a fucking cliche? I just wanted to know what it was like, why the hell you both needed to do it and why I haven't. I'm just as sad as both of you have been, surely I am.

Well, happy birthday, for what it's worth. It seems like we're beyond them now. I gave you a t-shirt this morning, short sleeved. What did I do that for? You wouldn't have worn it even if you didn't do this to yourself. What a joke.

Love and all the fear it insists on,
Dad

3/12/_____

Dear Dad,

We've been here, Dad. We've always been here. I'm wearing the t-shirt underneath my jumper. I do like it, honest.

Thank you for not making me show you my arm and for not looking at it while I'm asleep. I wouldn't like that and if you saw it I'd just lie. If I tell you about it in here then we never have to talk about it for real. I like that.

You want to know what cutting's like. Okay.

I've felt enough degrees of shame now that I can pick out the worst of them before they're over. I can still remember the shame running through me when I hit the window last year. Shame does not subside. It is exposed. It exposed itself openly as I hit the glass, and there was a terrible void between where I was and where you were, your face fell with mine, and I could not get that shame back unnoticed. I didn't know that I would hit the window again, and I didn't know that I would keep doing it until it broke, and I think I only found that out in the same moment you did. I may have heard the glass scatter across the kitchen floor before I knew what I had done. And there was silence the way there often is, which the pain in my hand tried to fill in for me. It did not succeed.

I left my boots by the door, which was a daft thing to do considering there was glass everywhere, but somehow

160

I passed between the kitchen and the hallway without stepping on it. I stretched out my hand on the way to my room. Quiet sounds - socks on carpet, the clearing of a throat - started to come back to me. I hadn't realised they had gone. Shame has a way of drowning them out.

I knew even before the glass broke that I would find myself upstairs, in the alcove by my window, taking a piece of the old broken mirror out from under the tray of a jewelry box. I had kept one shard, four inches or so long, that tended to come out in the aftermath of shame, or of fear, or of uselessness. I kept it clean with one of those cloths you get with a new pair of glasses, and I was always very careful taking it out. I set it down beside me and unfolded the cloth, exposing one corner to me at a time. One of them was getting a little dirty. I rolled up my sleeve. Back then it wasn't too difficult to find a good spot, and I picked out an area next to a few scars just below the inside of my elbow. I picked up the glass and shifted my grip so that I was holding it just above the point, with my index finger resting on the side, ready to push down. I let the glass touch my skin, and there was the briefest of moments where the glass held a temperature so low that it reminded me what season it was. It warmed almost immediately against my skin and I forgot the thought. I forget most thoughts when I'm cutting.

The glass caught a hair. I think I heard it. A pressure built and released from either breaking the hair or letting it go. I have a mole not far from where I was cutting, and I made sure I was a few millimetres away from it before I started, and I eyed a place I thought I would finish at that was further away than that. I don't know what it is like but I imagine cutting through a mole would hurt like fuck, and I don't much wish to have to take it. I looked back to where the glass was waiting, and I pushed lightly on it to start with. The skin whitened from where the blood was pushed away. I pushed a little harder and the skin dipped to where the faintest tip of the glass was buried. I let go. I wanted to see if I had broken the skin, but I hadn't. There was soreness somewhere and the skin reddened. I put the glass back on my arm and for some reason I looked away. I always look away. I pushed down harder with my finger and, although I wasn't sure if I had broken the skin yet, I ripped the glass across my arm.

No pain, not right away.

Deep breaths.

I looked back. Sometimes looking at the cut afterwards could be privately embarrassing, when only a hesitant cat-scratch was left. Those are the ones that hurt more for some reason. I managed more than that that day, and deeper cuts don't bleed as quickly as they do on the TV. There were a few seconds, maybe twenty, where I could just look at the underside of my skin. It was strangely peaceful. It was pale in there, with the thinnest of red lines scattered within it. Blood crept in from the corners, the way people slowly cry. It met in the middle and filled what was only a millimetre or two deep, and an inch or two long.

Blood cools incredibly quickly. It was only seconds after the cut filled with blood that it began to overflow, and then a trail of blood streaked down my forearm towards the wrist. A chilled tickle moved along with it. I played around, posing my arm in different positions, seeing where I could get the trails to divert to without dropping any blood to the carpet. It is in moments like that one that I am completely lost, forgetting everything, blinded to the embers of emotion. The feeling began to throb from under the skin, and it reminded me that cutting yourself hurts one way or another, but I knew I had a few moments left before it became only pain.

I got some tissue and pressed it against the cut. I began to remember again that I had broken the window, and I remembered your face blankly. Your eyes, Dad, your fallen eyes, took their place in my mind as each notch of soreness came back to my fist. My fist, the cut, and your face took their positions in trying to hurt me the most.

I lifted the tissue. Just some smudges and a wound.

I dug my nails in and I winced.

Dear Eleanor,

I woke up today to a note on the kitchen table. 'Dad, I'm going somewhere else today. Keep warm. Love from Every,' with a kiss. I did what she told me. I kept warm. I lit candles by all the seats I knew I would use so there would be a little something of you wherever I went, but I kept the heat on because she told me to. There's a lot that she knows.

She knows how you felt. She cuts herself. I hope so much that she doesn't get as far into all of that as you did. It killed you after all. I'd tell her to stop before it goes too far but it already has because it has happened at all. It kills me to think of what she must be feeling, it makes me die every day, but I know I can't do anything to stop it because you're the one who knows how to do that. I should have been the one to go, Eleanor, and then she could have become me instead. Someone unremarkable, and incredibly safe. Someone who's just there. But I dreamed her into her own world, didn't I? How was she ever going to be just someone?

I can imagine her cutting your name into her skin. Es and Ls all over her. Is that all the consolation left for her? Your name on her skin?

That doesn't seem like much of a consolation.

6/12/_____

I'll take whatever I can get.

I wish I'd been inside in the cold. I probably wouldn't have hurt myself today if you had done it for me.

Dear Every,

The pictures, the memorisations, that I have made of you this year have been from a distance, and they have stilled to the point where they are nearly photographs. I have one particular image of you in my mind, where you were in the kitchen and I was at the foot of the stairs, and the doorframes between us layered up across each other to border you. Grey tones blended. Light filled the kitchen through the replacement window and it rippled around your silhouette.

That is all I see of you, all it seems.

I clean that window obsessively.

I hope you are okay.

You looked okay, from there.

Love,
Dad

3/12/_____

Dear Dad,

I have a different picture. It was the end of October. It was Halloween. And I'd got myself all dressed up. I wore this torn black shawl over a vest, and the cotton draped like raven wings. I had cut myself in the alcove, gashes up my arms, and I smeared the blood all over rather than cleaning it up. The wounds seeped under the crust.

I walked a few of the streets. It was darkening and the kids were out but the blood was still on show. I walked with my arms turned outwards, and I watched for people looking but I'm not sure anyone did. I guess the blood blurred into the dark. It was cold. I carried a cigarette. I walked with my mouth open and the smoke poured out.

I was a real picture. I was a joke, but I was a picture.

Eve x

Dear Eleanor,

Every has been waiting for today for months now, maybe a whole year, I know she has. It's been cold here all day for that reason. I feel like, honestly, I might be better off just leaving these letters to you behind now, but for as long as the fifth exists I want to keep doing them, just in case I regret leaving one out one day. I can't take regretting much more than I already do. I was up today very early to make sure it was as cold as I could make it. A cold breakfast and no candles lighted until it was almost Every's usual time to wake up, about seven thirty. My goodness, I'd forgotten how cold this place could get. I think my breath stuck to the walls like spiderwebs. Little pieces of you were caught in them, and the only creature to be seen was me. The webs spawned in every crevice. Every time I breathed out I followed it to the newest one, a patch of frost on something I could pretend came from me and you.

Then I remembered the one thing that ever did, and I went upstairs to make an 'accidental' noise to wake her up into this incredible cold that she has missed out on for the last two years.

She did not wake. She already had. I looked inside, and everything was as immaculate as ever. You have a very tidy child, Eleanor, but she's a damn evasive one as well, because she had woken up before me and fucked off completely and left me here alone in my own damn cold and done it all on purpose.

God damn it.

6/12/_____

Dad, I'm sorry. I wanted to stay home but I couldn't sleep all night worrying about it. I hurt myself a lot while I was out, just to show my body what I think of it. It knows. It just won't ever leave me the fuck alone.

And yeah, you're right. God damn it. And I pray he keeps damning it until our next letters.

x

3/12/_____

Dear Dad,

There's nothing here. I'm writing next to Mum's memory box on your bedroom floor with the pen you keep in it, and there's no letter from yesterday. The others are here, all of them, but you didn't write to me on my birthday. Oh my God.

It's the first time this has happened - that I've opened the box and there's nothing new for me to read. And so I guess my gift next year will be incomplete. Well, we nearly made it. I suppose you're still upset with me. I will get to that.

This is not the first time I have sat on the floor alone and quiet. It's funny the things you notice when you focus on the quiet - did you know my breathing stutters? It's on the exhale, and it sounds like there's something in the way of the air. It happens almost every time and my breathing sounds sparse when it doesn't. I must have spent hours of my life sitting with my back to my bed, hiding from nothing, hanging my head so that my hair brushes against the blood when I'm bleeding. It's doing it now although I haven't cut - yet - today. I'm swinging my hair back and forth just a little. It tickles. Today my back is against your bed, which smells different to mine. You are out so I guess I have some time to sit in here. It feels not too far from some distant, weeping embrace between you and I to have the wood from your bedframe dig at my spine. I wish you had written. It turns out Mum isn't all I can miss.

Without a letter, the scars on my arm look a lot like writing. I can get lost looking into them. I can get lost looking into the clusters of tiny marks from when I didn't know what I was doing, and I can get lost looking into the pinkened tissue from when I really did get in there.

I wish I could count them. I wouldn't know where to start. I can't find the first ones anymore, lost and faded under layers, scratching each other out. There's a group just off to the side, where if you look at them right they all bend in the same direction. That's the closest I've come to cutting skin at a curve, and if you can actually do that then it's news to me. And they reach right into the thick of it, to where this bulbous gash that's a few weeks old sticks out. It probably needed stitches but I managed to tape it up with those little strips you get from the pharmacy. The cut was still wet under my top when I bought them. It stuck to my sleeve. It's pretty ugly now. I guess most of it is just cross hatching. Cutting across scars hurts. You can feel the glass slip across the scar tissue and it leaves cuts behind that are so much thinner than the others, but if you can avoid the harshest scars then it's not too bad. It's getting harder to do that.

If I look too long it starts to fuck with me. Mum used to take me for walks, and there was a game we played. We'd be on one of the streets near the house, and we'd imagine that the power lines above the roads were staves.

We'd wait for the birds to come and settle on them, and then we'd pretend they were the notes. And Mum would sing them to me. I tried, but even now I can only halfway read music, so I just copied her. Black birds were crotchets and white ones were minims, and then we took some creative license depending on how close they were to each other. We could spend half a day humming those to each other, and when we got home Mum would ask me what my favourite ones were, and she would play them to me. And now it looks like my arm is covered in staves, and whatever marks happen to be around fill in for the music, and my head keeps circling around the melodies.

I can't even remember why half the cuts are there. I know a lot of them are because of you. But they all make so much noise now that they drown you out, the way you've drowned yourself out of my life, and you out of your own, for the most part. I don't even know how you like to fill your time, or if you like it filled at all. I think it's a consequence of you still being here that I don't remember you as well as I do Mum. I don't make the effort. The moments I cut myself, I guess, are the moments I know you are still here.

I guess I was having a thing about dads in August, because I ended up tracking down Mum's. I'd thought about it before, since you told me about him in a letter, and he turned out pretty easy to find. I kind of enjoyed the detective work to be honest. He had moved since back when you knew him, and it was a couple of hours on a train to get there but the journey down south was okay. I only took a backpack with a book and some water in it, and that was enough to get me there. Thankfully it was a decent day out when I arrived, because he lived about an hour's walk from the train station and I didn't have the money for a taxi or the patience for the bus. You walk in the road down there and the houses have names instead of numbers.

The map told me to take the coastal path, but I knew what my head fills with when I'm near the water so I went inland, even though it meant taking a couple of wrong turns. I'm not great with direction. I guess I don't go to enough places. I'd imagined when you get to the middle of nowhere that everyone says Hi, but it turns out they ignore you all the same. They just seem to take their time about it.

Grandad's place was a good few minutes' walk up a hill. Loose gravel and tight turns all over the place - it must be murder in the rain. The shade was such a relief that I zigzagged a few times to stay in it, which really just meant that when I got there I was even more out of breath than I had to be. The house was a single storey and without a fence, but the land all blended into the rest out there so he might have had more than it looked like, though if he did, he wasn't doing much with it. There weren't even sheep. I thought everywhere in the country had sheep.

The road turned to a track, which turned again into a makeshift doorstep. I hadn't really thought until I knocked that not everyone stays home as much as we do, and that maybe he'd be out. It was a few seconds wait, but then the sound of stifled shuffling started, and it loudened until it stopped, and then the creaks and clicks of readying a door to open took over, and my mouth had to wonder what words to use. I'd forgotten to plan them. I always plan them. I heard the saliva work its way around my tongue as it ran through its repertoire.

Grandad was older than I thought. It was either that or a shitty life. He was maybe seventy or a little less. His skin only had yellow to keep it from going grey, and his eyes had turned near enough translucent. He was kind of short too. Shitloads of hair though - he probably needed it cut, or even just to give it a good comb.

'Hello?' he said. He had more in his voice than I was ready for, some kind of slow-paced clarity. It was really deep too. Rumbling.

'Hi. Hello.' My eyes flickered downwards a little. I heard him breathe just as slowly as he had spoken. I said, 'Do you... do you know who I am?'

He shook his head while he looked me all over. 'No,' he said. 'But I suppose you know me?'

I said, 'I'm Every,' and then I shut my damn mouth.

'No,' he said, and I readied my eyes to shut them too, but he kept looking, and he lurched forward with his neck, and then he pulled it back and he said, 'Christ, so you are.' And he moved quicker than I thought he could, and he pulled the door open further, and he said, 'Come in.' He crammed himself against the wall so I could get inside. 'Do come in.' The hallway was dim, and the wallpaper was a faint rose colour all the way along. There was a door on each side just ahead of me, great white wooden ones, and they were closed. At the end of the hallway was the kitchen. The table was in the centre, his chair to the side with a single glass of water and a newspaper in front of it. The table was wood - proper wood, not the kind we have. There were no stairs. One of the closed rooms must have been where he slept.

I stood barely inside, wondering if this was a shoes on or shoes off kind of place. 'Go through,' he said kindly, so I guessed shoes on was fine. I walked through and my boots clattered on the wooden floor. When I got to the kitchen the sound deadened on the tile and I found a corner to stand in. Grandad followed me in and stood in the doorway, looking at me all eyes-wide like I was a new species. I suppose that's how you used to look at me. 'Sit down,' he said, holding his arm out towards the chair nearest to me. I shuffled towards it and dropped my bag. I sat down.

'Can I get you some tea?' he asked. 'Do you drink tea?'

'Oh, no. Thank you.'

I actually would have loved some tea but I wasn't ready for the question. I couldn't remember the last time I'd been in someone else's kitchen. I didn't realise how different another house could smell. Like oak and woodsmoke. It was intoxicating. Or at least it threw me.

'Something to eat? It must have been a long trip.'

'I'm fine. Thank you.'

He sat in front of his newspaper and pushed it away. He put his hands on the table, both palms down, his elbows hanging low off the edge.

'So,' he said. 'What brings you here?'

You'd think I'd have an answer.

'It's so good to see you,' he said. 'I've never seen you. You must be, what, fifteen, sixteen now?'

'Sixteen.'

'Gosh. Sixteen. Sixteen years. My, that time's disappeared. Did your dad tell you where I was?'

I shook my head. 'I don't think he knows where you are.'

'And I can't imagine he wonders.' He spoke so slowly. 'No, he never liked me.' He left a silence there and I watched his eyelids tighten through it. The creases on his forehead coarsened. I think he'd spent a lot of time like that.

'I don't much blame him,' he said. 'Not really.'

Suddenly it felt like all I'd gone there to do was upset the poor man.

'Does anyone else live here?' I asked.

'No. I came here after your grandma died. It's just me here. It's so good to see you, Every. It's so good to say your name. Your father thought of it, if I remember rightly.'

I nodded. 'I think so,' I said.

'I try not to say it. You don't realise how often you say the same words in your life. Your name's all over the place, even in the dullest day. It's near enough everywhere. See.'

There was some air let out of him, not far off a laugh. I got the impression he was only used to laughing to himself.

'Every, can I ask you what your father has told you about me?'

I didn't say anything right away. It must have sounded to him like I was putting off answering, but I was running through in my head if there had actually been any times when you'd mentioned him. I don't think there were. 'I actually don't think he's talked about you.'

Grandad's head bobbed slowly as he breathed. 'In a way, Every, that's a relief. There's not a lot of good to say, you see. I always thought you never came because you hated me. And I was too scared to ask to visit.'

'I don't hate you,' I said. 'I don't know you.'

'And you're here because you want to know me?'

'To be honest I'm not sure why I'm here.'

'I see. Sometimes we just find ourselves places, don't we? Well, I'd like to know how life has been to you. If you will tell me.'

If the request didn't cut me, the politeness damn well did. You've always told me I didn't cry as a child but the tears threatened an appearance then. 'I wouldn't know what to say,' I said, through the kind of voice that bubbles and then chokes. I felt the most intense and sudden urge to break into pieces small enough to rain.

'It's okay, Every. Forget, forget I asked. How is your dad faring these days?'

'Oh, I don't know. I don't know. Probably not good. He doesn't talk to me about… he doesn't talk to me about much at all, really.'

'That's a shame,' he said. 'You're sure I can't get you anything?'

I shook my head. I stared across the table at him, at this man I'd barely thought of in my life, whose kindness appeared the type that would persist, whoever it was that was sat at his table. He did not appear to be the bitter drunk you have told me about. Well, I guess he had time to change.

'I imagined you more resentful,' I said.

One of his hands clawed up slowly. Arthritic.

'Sorry,' I said. 'I didn't mean it like that.'

'It's okay,' he said. 'I am resentful. That's the honest truth. I am.'

'Of Dad?'

'Hardly. His hatred of me is as near to justified as hatred gets. I'm resentful of myself, because I deserve it.' Grandad sounded wise to me, and I guess I'm still young enough to mistake wisdom for infallibility. I believed him. Even as he spoke to me I had no intention of asking him to go on. It just seemed cruel. But I'm so low on conversational practise that the question just came out.

'Will you tell me what happened?'

'I would be so pleased to.' He said it quickly, like he'd been saving up the words for the chance. 'The trouble is, if you're after clear answers, there's no one here who can give them to you.'

'What do you mean?'

'Well. I was a very weak young man, Every. I suppose you could say I'm a weak old one too.'

'I wouldn't say that.'

'That's kind,' he said nodding. 'And I was selfish. Your grandma and I married young. Everyone did back then. I don't think I was a bad husband. I went to work. We weren't unhappy. Life was fairly simple, but I grew too used to it. There wasn't much in the way of obligation, you see. I just had to come home from work and be sure to shine my shoes every once in a while. Iron a shirt. Time passed agreeably, for the most part. We hadn't planned on being parents, or even discussed it, but your mother was born one year in the spring. We nearly called her Spring, in fact. At first, I was around often enough. I fed her. Taught her to walk. We played together as a family. We had a pond at the end of the garden, which your mother loved, so we spent several afternoons there with a picnic of apples and sandwiches. But I did struggle. At first I withdrew a little. I took extra shifts at work that we didn't need, and then I realised it was just as well to say I'd taken the work, and just bum around for an evening. So of course you end up in the pub.'

He looked up at me for the first time in minutes. 'I'm sorry it's such a typical story. I just gave in.'

'I'm sure you did your best.'

'If all I had been was a drinker, I'm sure your father would have forgiven me. That's life for a lot of people. But I discovered very quickly that my aptitude for self control was entirely absent. The ensuing years turned into a constant scraping of bottle caps. I'm told that your grandma's parents used to drive past our house on Sundays, just to check that we weren't on fire. They did not trust me. They were right not to. I was angry, often, and of the few things I remember of those years, your mother's frightened face burns my conscience the most. I know I neglected her. I hope I never raised a hand to her, but Every, I remember so little. I expect I did. The foggiest memories - they can be the cruellest. I last saw your mother when she was barely any older than you are. Whatever I did to her, it was enough for her to stay away. Your grandma died soon after. Your father probably knows more of my life than I do, truthfully. I can't have been good. I can't have been.'

'It was a long time ago,' I said.

'Was it?'

I guess it's easy to say that when you're a fucking child.

'I don't even remember meeting him,' he said. 'I know I did, though. Drinking memories away seemed a sound idea at the time. Well, I stopped eventually. Don't get muddled up in all of that, Every. There's nothing there.

You know, I found out that your mother had died in an email. It read only of politeness. I wonder if I'd have known at all if I hadn't worked out how to use the damn computer. Doubtful.'

'You missed her funeral.'

'Yes. Yes I did. Another shame.'

'I'm sorry.'

'Did you go?' he asked.

'Yes.'

'I once thought of visiting her grave. But I didn't know how to find it without asking your dad. I still don't know.'

'I can tell you where it is.'

'I would like that. I did go back home once. I remember I walked to the end of the pier. I remember crying, just streams of tears. I passed a number of people but none of them spoke to me. But I was crying. I felt lost. Streams of tears. I daren't go back again. No. This will do. I have a garden here. What use is visiting a grave anyway?'

'I don't know. Dad doesn't go. Well, the house may as well be the grave these days.'

'Oh. That's telling.'

'I suppose he might go. I don't suppose he'd tell me to be honest.'

'What do you remember of her? I'd like to know what she was like, as a mother.'

I could have told him the truth, all of it, that the memories I've kept the most vivid are the ones that would terrify him. I could have told him about how I watched mum's scars amass more and more. I could have told him about seeing the pain in her stomach double her over out of the blue. And I could have told him that I watched her die. I couldn't give him those pictures of her. Those are mine. I'm sure they are among yours. But I didn't want them to be his, even if he was part of the reason they existed. 'She was lovely,' I said, which was true if nothing else. 'She was always good to me. She taught me to play the piano.'

'I remember her learning.'

'I don't play much these days.'

'You must. It's a beautiful instrument. If I had one here I'd learn myself.'

'I just remember she gave good hugs. She always wanted to be close to me.'

'Ah. More like your grandma than me.'

'She liked to find things to do that were free. I don't think we had much money. We went walking a lot. Went to the beach. She loved to swim.'

'Did she?' His eyes opened wide. 'That's funny. I don't think we ever got her to go swimming more than a couple of times as a child. She would never go in. She'd just sit on the side of the pool. I guess you grow into these things.'

'We used to swim together. Well, she used to pull me along. I really enjoyed that.'

'There's a beach not far from here.'

'Yeah. I don't really like going anymore.'

'Fair enough.'

'Too many memories, you know.'

'I know. It's nice thinking of her teaching you to swim.' He put his fingers to his head. The tips yellowed from the pushing. 'I like thinking of her like that. Hair wet and pushed back. Hands on yours. Maybe she would dive down. Come back up smiling. Yes. Come back up smiling.' He kept pressing on his head. 'I don't remember seeing that very much - her smiling.' He kept pushing. He held that shape for most of a minute. I watched him the whole time, his cheeks occasionally flickering, the exhalations so deep and the inhale imperceptible. He had swollen knuckles, and stubble the shade of chalk. Suddenly I felt very, very young.

'Will you be visiting again, Every?'

'Yes,' I said, and my stomach got hot. I felt like I had lied.

'Good.'

Grandad showed me the garden that afternoon. If he hadn't called it that I wouldn't have thought it was one.

I thought about Grandad all the way home, except for when I thought about Mum. It was hardly any time after the train started going that I began to get flashes in my mind of the photograph I still had of her. I kept it in a drawer, as hidden as the pieces of glass. The flashes were brief at first, like the white dots left behind after you screw your eyes shut, but the photo prolonged its appearances the nearer I got to home. It was late in the evening by the time I got to the front door, and the thought of that picture had become vivid enough by then that I may as well have been walking with it hanging in front of my face. I opened the door as narrowly as I could so as to slip inside and get up to my room. I let the night pass with me awake in it, until there was just enough morning light coming through the curtain for me to dig out the photo without turning the light on. I hadn't looked at it or touched it in years. I could tell which side was the back because it felt like paper, and the front felt shiny although it wasn't all that smooth. It was a little creased at the edges and it had that curve across the surface that pictures had when you used to get them developed at the chemist. I ran my fingers across the photo, feeling for any signs of Mum, as though she was braille. Nothing. I sat in the alcove and watched the photo until my eyes adjusted enough to the light to see her outline, her narrow face and tidy hair, and eventually her button eyes. As the light heaved in I watched her face come to life, and memories gushed. I remembered Mum at the piano, every few bars looking at me instead of the keys. I remembered us out for walks. I remembered the three of us in the living room with the TV on mute. I remembered her dying but not nearly as much as I remembered us all living, and I realised how long ago and gone it all suddenly felt. I thought about how long ago it was since Grandad had seen her, and I wondered what would come back to him if he had the same picture in his hands. My fingers clutched around the photo at the thought, reluctant to give up any little link I had to her, but what use had a photo been, locked and most days forgotten in the bottom of a drawer?

And then came my mistake, my most recent one anyway. As much as I thought Grandad might like to see it, I couldn't let it go without showing it to you first.

I ate breakfast across the table from you, chewing my food at the front of my mouth. You sipped your coffee slowly. You never look out of place without a phone or a newspaper to stare into, and while I fiddled with the tabletop while I ate, you just sat there, monolithic, waiting for the day to happen if it must.

The last of my toast disappeared into my throat and I gargled 'Dad?' over it.

'Mm,' you said, replacing your coffee cup on the table.

'I found something.'

Your mouth hardly moved: 'What is it?'

I reached back and pulled the photo out of my pocket. I held it in my lap and I felt my fingers quiver. 'I found it.' Voice too. I pushed the picture across the table. 'I thought you'd want to see.'

The picture was facing me. Your shoulders lifted as you breathed. 'You know full well I don't want to see that,' you said. You looked down at your fingers, or to the cracks in the tabletop, or maybe at nothing at all so long as it wasn't the picture.

'But she looks nice, doesn't she?' What hope.

'Every, I don't want to see. Where did you get it?'

'I found it.'

'Bullshit.'

'What do you mean?' Your face had arranged the shadows of its features masterfully.

'I never kept any. Don't even think I took any.' Your jaw chewed at nothing. 'Where did you get it?'

'I - I don't know.'

Before I saw it, your fist had landed on the table so hard that I sat back, and the photo turned from the force so that mum wasn't facing either of us anymore. 'How long have you had that?' you shouted, your eyes on mine more than I had seen them for months. 'How long?'

'She gave it to me,' I said, and I tried not to sound scared. What I wouldn't have given for a razor or a shard.

'If you don't get that away from me...'

Veins grew spikes. You pushed the picture across the table, and it got crumpled up as you did. I don't know if you did that on purpose.

'Just get it away from me.'

I picked it up, stood up, and backed away, holding the picture so that it faced me. My hands are small - I had to use both of them to cover it up completely.

'If I see that again,' you said, 'I'll burn it.'

'Okay.'

I ran back upstairs with Mum's picture held tight. I heard a plate smash. Cupboards slammed shut, something was hit, and I heard you swearing louder the longer I listened. I bet that's what Grandad sounded like when he was younger. It was more than I'd heard out of you for days, and more than I cared to hear from you from then until who knows when - well, until today.

That photo was in the post to Grandad within hours. And now I don't have a picture of Mum and I don't have a letter from you.

It's too much to miss.

Eve x

Dear Eleanor,

It was some days after you died that I first trawled the house for a picture of you. Most of what I saw in those first few days was Every's broken down face, her skin strained, always, in the absence of her crying. When she did not need me, either from solitude or sleep, I slept myself, and so those days passed largely empty, and not soon enough. I dreamed of you, of course. My mind seemed to pick out things that I didn't know I remembered, and it reached back further and further into our lives, into our one life, until I watched us as barely more than children. I watched us walk city streets and country gardens. We used to walk a lot. My, how we ambled. We had no place to go and nothing to do, so we just spent our time near each other, which was always enough for me. In each dream the colours in every part of you intensified as everything that wasn't you slowly greyed out, and before long, every time I closed my eyes, your face burst in front of me like a firework.

I was right, even then, that those images would never leave me, but the fear that they would take over any ability I might have had to set them aside led to the secret wish that I had just one picture of you, only to ground me, to reset the image, to save a cruel imagination from doing a real number on me. My avoidance of photographs had always been forensic, but yours, I knew, had not. You accommodated it kindly, selflessly, and I doubt you were ever comfortable with it. Until a few months after you met me, you kept photos like anybody else. Apparently everyone does that. And so I always figured you had some old pictures hidden away, and it would have been downright sinister of me to expect you to get rid of them. It was bad enough that part of me wanted it. It was while the remembrances of you burned at the back of my eyes that I realised you were right. And it was with childlike embarrassment, perhaps the beginnings of regret, that I turned out every drawer and searched the back of every cupboard until I found one half-full photo album in the cupboard by your side of the bed. I put it on the nightstand and opened it. The pages were coated with plastic and they had cardboard inserts. I guess those things are meant to last. On the first page there were pictures of you and your family - your parents and some other people I couldn't place. It looked like someone's birthday. Possibly yours. You were a kid. Everyone wore these shabby smiles. The next few pages were almost all you. I guess you really liked pictures, and I'm a little ashamed that I didn't really know that. It looked like life wasn't always as tormenting to you as I knew it could be. Sometimes you just liked to goof around, like in the picture of you wearing elephant ears to the supermarket. I bet you got some looks that day. Well, good. And then there were the pictures of Every. She was just as I remembered her, somehow stoic. It was strange to see them. I knew you must have had pictures of yourself, but I was not expecting to see Every in that album, and I am afraid to say that if I am honest, I felt a little bit betrayed by that.

And then there were pictures of me.

It was such a simple motion, swiping the album from the nightstand to the bin.

I would be lying to you if I said there were never times when I regret throwing it out, and I would be lying again if I said I didn't feel the back of my neck swell up when I'm searching the back of a drawer for batteries, as I realise it's not just a thought that I might find a stray photograph there, but a hope.

And so I found myself awfully surprised at the anger I felt when Every showed me the picture of you that she had kept. I think I showed that anger. I imagine it looked somewhat like I was upset that she had it, and although that's partly true, it was seeing that picture that rekindled my great concern that I had made a mistake in never keeping any. Gosh, it was so good to see you. But I can't have regret. I can't have regret.

I can apologise. The rest of that day was spent wondering how on earth to apologise for shouting, when I don't believe I have ever shouted at her before. I'm not sure I've shouted since I was a child. I figured the surest way was to just say sorry, but what an embarrassment that it was something I had to work out. And what a floodgate it could open: Every, I'm sorry for shouting. I'm sorry for being frightened to talk to you. I'm sorry you don't have pictures of your mum. I'm sorry you don't have your mum. I'm sorry I don't hug you. I'm sorry I can't stop you hurting yourself. I'm sorry I have probably caused you to hurt yourself. I'm sorry it wasn't me who died. I'm sorry that my tendency to keep emotion away keeps you away too. I'm sorry I've never apologised before. I'm sorry in case I don't apologise again. I'm sorry for everything you remember but that I have forgotten. I'm sorry too for everything I remember. I'm sorry that I don't have it within my capacity to make you happy. Or anyone.

It was at around seven o'clock that evening that I mustered up the will to go to Every's room. I hadn't seen her at all since the argument. I knocked, and I waited. It must have been quite the surprise - I don't knock often. I heard her moving around inside but she didn't come to the door, so I knocked again and said her name. She still didn't come, so I knocked and pushed the door open a little. 'Every?' I said. She was moving across the room towards the alcove.

'Mm,' she said.

I stepped inside. 'I wanted to talk to you.'

'Mm.'

I stood still and watched her. She was stumbling as she walked. 'Are you okay?' I asked.

'I'm just putting the light on,' she said. She was nowhere near the light switch and the light was on already. She touched the wall. She spoke very slowly. I quickly looked around the room. I thought maybe there was some drink out. I didn't know of her drinking, but then again I didn't know of much. I couldn't see anything. It didn't smell of drink. The drawers were closed and the tabletops were tidy. She more or less fell into the alcove. I watched. She did not watch back. Her breathing was heavy and I could hear it from where I stood. I waited for what felt like minutes, letting the speech I wanted to give slip away. Every's eyes were closed. I suppose it may have just been sleep. I went over to her, pulled up a stool from the desk, and sat right beside her. There was blood on her cuff. I pulled her sleeve back carefully. It was hard to tell how bad the cuts were because her top had smudged the blood so much, but they looked fresh to me. I got some wipes and cleaned them up the best I could. I threw them away in my bedroom bin instead of hers. When it seemed they had stopped bleeding, I pulled her sleeve back down the way she likes it. I sat there until nearly morning. A couple of hours of sleep afterwards would do me. I didn't tell her anything while I sat there. Wiping her arm was all the apology I could give her.

I apologise now nearly every night. I will apologise as much as she needs me to.

Love,
David

December 1st _____

Dear Every,

I'm making a vigil of my last letter to you. It's the night before your eighteenth birthday - it's the hour before, actually - and in a few hours this letter will be in your hands. A lot of other things have been in them these eighteen years, and a lot more has been out of them, but they're on their way to you, my love, and I can't wait to give them to you.

Your childhood is almost gone. What was it like? Tell me honestly. I did try to make it something worth having. I hope you know that, at least.

I am sorry that last year's letter is missing. I'm afraid I didn't write one. As far as your recollection is concerned, a lot of that year didn't happen, but it still exists in the sum of your feelings and I think it's best we leave it there, in both of ours. I will share one thing though, as I know you remember it, so I know the telling won't threaten your consciousness with more than it needs. I was sitting in your room on a Tuesday night, cleaning your wounds while you slept in the scent of wine. The bottle was on the side and you had drunk nearly all of it. I lifted the tissue from your cuts. The wound underneath filled quickly with blood, and I slapped the tissue back on and pressed hard. You winced but you did not wake. It was only two more minutes that I held it for, but it felt like forever, as I simply spent the time admiring you. You slept with your brow slightly furrowed, and your breath sounded more ruffled than your voice. I suppose that may have been the wine. I thought it was nice how your hair was tied so neatly, and I'm afraid I ruined it a little by stroking it. I felt your scars. They were raised and rough in places and so smooth in others that I could have sworn my finger slid on them. I had never quite appreciated how many of them there were. The fat ones take centre stage and it is only when you push them aside like a curtain that the smaller, and the thinner, and the nearly invisible ones show themselves. Every time I moved my head to see another in the light, a handful more would appear, and a handful more again. I felt the breath from my nose on the back of my hand, and the shame in my spine. There were hundreds, I'd say.

I checked your cuts again and the bleeding had started to slow. There were pieces of tissue stuck in the blood. You whimpered. I threw the tissue away and went to the bathroom to get a damp cloth to clean you up with. On my way out of your room I heard you groan. On my way back, you woke. You woke with so sudden a wail that I thought you'd had a nightmare. I hurried back and when I got to your room you were clutching at your stomach, chin in the chest.

'Every, what's wrong?'

Not only did you have to contend with the pain, but with me being so to near it. I don't know which was worse. Your head snapped to face me and I will never forget how contorted and desperate it was, even briefly, and how your instinct seemed to be to suck all expression back in. You failed.

'What is it?' I asked.

'Noth-,' you said. You might have said the rest of the word too but it vanished amongst the groaning.

I pulled my phone out and called an ambulance.

'No,' you said. Your nails scratched me. I think it was probably meant for the phone.

I told the ambulance where to come.

'Fucking put it down.' Well, you said enough of it for me to work the rest out.

They saw us pretty quickly at the hospital. They let me stay with you. They hooked you up to some tubes and some wires and you squirmed as they did it.

'Where does it hurt, Every?' the doctor asked.

'It doesn't.' You tried not to clutch the top of your stomach. The doctor touched it. He pressed and you flinched.

'I know,' he said. 'Have you been drinking, Every?'

You didn't say anything.

'Have you taken anything?'

You didn't say anything then either.

'It's important you tell us if you have.'

'She's been drinking,' I said. 'Wine.' I kept my eyes on the doctor. 'It was in her room. I don't know about anything else.'

'Right,' he said.

A nurse brought something to the doctor and he read it in the corridor. He came back and sat down. Doctors don't just sit down for anything. 'Every, you've been here before, haven't you? After taking too many tablets?' His tone was softer, his words slower.

You didn't say anything. I sat down too, knees practically at my ears. The doctor looked at me. 'I'm sorry if you didn't know that,' he said. I shook my head, more like waved it.

'Have you done that tonight, Every?' I don't know why he had to say your name every time he spoke to you.

You didn't say anything.

'Can I talk to Every alone for a moment?'

I nodded. I hadn't really finished shaking my head yet so God knows what that looked like. From the corridor I could hear the doctor's voice but not what it said. I couldn't hear yours at all. I waited two or three minutes. Nurses have a habit of rushing around and every time one went by me, I thought they were rushing to you. They were not. The curtain opened and the doctor came out. I noticed how blackened it was under his eyes. 'What did she do?' I asked.

'She won't say. I'm sending her blood for tests. I'll be back when I've got the results.'

I closed the curtain behind me and then I sat back down. I can't imagine you looked at me, but I wouldn't know because I didn't look at you either. We held our shapes like statues. I'd been in that hospital with your mother I don't how many times. Once is enough to be there with you. You know the pace our lives pass at - swatting thoughts away is usually something I can find the time for, but I practically had my head in a hive of them in the hospital. When were you there before? Was it only once? Would they tell me? Was it my fault? I was sure it was my fault. Would they tell me that?

They really ought not have so many clocks at the hospital. The passing of a couple of hours stretched itself out like putty. By the time the doctor came back, I was shaking my leg from needing the toilet so much. He closed the curtain behind him. I sat up straight, palms on thighs.

'The good news is there's no lasting damage.' He didn't say it much like good news. Every has taken aspirin. Quite a lot of it. That and alcohol don't mix well. She's going to have a bad stomach for a day or two, but that's about it. I should tell you, if she keeps this up she might not stay so lucky.'

Don't I know it.

'Every, we can offer you someone to talk to. If you would like.'

You didn't say anything.

He asked me.

I didn't say anything either.

For the longest time this year, for all of it really, I have been scared that tomorrow morning would come and you wouldn't be in a much better state than that, or that you would be in a worse one completely. Then I wouldn't know what to do with these. But, fortunately, there is more of you in this December than there was in the last, and I haven't caught you with too many stomach aches. Hopefully when you get these in a few hours I'll be giving you parts of the person you've always been, and you'll see her in yourself again. Heal those aches. She's wonderful, Every, she really is.

She's my daughter. She is not perfect. I do regret that your imperfections and my incessant worries are such a large part of the gift I am about to give you, but those have been our lives, Every, those have been our lives. I only started to look these over, for the first time, in the hours before this. Until today, your letters have sat here, in your mother's memory box, which now I will show you, unread. They have had a lot to say, or at least I meant them to. They are, of course, only attempts to say what was in my heart in the moments before I wrote each word, and trying to translate such a thing is always destined to fail because once the pen touches the paper those moments are gone. I did try, though, and it's in the trying, not the words, that I hope you'll find my love for you, and how unchanged it has been since you were born, and before.

Yes, your heart. I must apologise. These last couple of years have been rotten, and there have been some confessions, but now that you have read these, you know the recording of your mother's heart is really yours. This confession makes right everything you have ever done to me, or worse, to yourself. Anything you still do. All of the things you still do. I have never done anything so cruel as telling you that lie, and please be sure that whatever sadness is going through your heart as you are finding this out, the same has been bleeding in mine since the day I told it. I won't ask your forgiveness. I don't hear your heart's beating coming from your room very often, as though in some way you have outgrown it, but on the evenings I do hear it, I close my eyes and imagine you are as close to me as you were when we recorded it.

You still have your moments. I don't think they will go away. But the fading looks that plagued our last year have mostly evaporated, and your arm isn't getting too much worse anymore, and everything seems to be slowing down to a speed that, actually, I like. We can move forward if we hold it, I really think we can.

It is almost midnight, almost your eighteenth birthday, and I wonder what you are doing and if you are seeing it in asleep. It's the best way. There are no sounds coming from your bedroom, and it is like it used to be. I'll be sleeping soon myself, but I am going to wait for these next few minutes to pass because this is a day I have been waiting for as long as I have waited for anything. The last words I will write will be about your mother.

Believe, Every, that if she was here and had watched all of this, all that you have done to yourself, she would still be proud of you this morning. And believe that you would have shown her something she had never seen. She never believed herself special, but watching what you have lived through, the pride and the love she would feel, she would also have to feel for herself, because ultimately you came from her. You would have saved her her memory of herself, and that's something most of us never get right. Just like, even though it was only for a little while, you saved her life.

December 2nd _____

It is finally here - happy birthday, Every.

My love, and my life, until one outlives the other,
Your father

(Oh my God I have a grown up daughter!)

December 2nd _____

Dear Eleanor,

There have been very few moments when I have thought another death would be a mercy, and right, if it happened just then. I can hear Every crying through the wall and she is making no attempt to disguise it. One of those moments was this morning. I slept very lightly, and I went downstairs excited at the smell of the mushrooms she was making for me, with her letters folded in an envelope in my hand. I went straight to her, a very faint smell of smoke on her, and as I leaned over to wish her a happy birthday, I heard her arm burn against the pan, and then her eyes met mine, sad eyes on sad eyes, and I saw her expression stay the same, stay vacant, and unknowing of pain. She leaned against the stove because she had to lean against something, she could hardly stand. I pushed her away from it, and I would say she collapsed on the floor but really she just sat on it, and she was crying, I think, dry tears. How could she let this be the day she turned back on herself? I dropped the letters when I pushed her, and they landed beside her. 'What's this?' she asked, with no pain in her voice at all. I picked them back up.

I left her in the kitchen, as she was, and she stayed there a long while. Maybe half of the day. The mushrooms had been cold for a long, long time before I went back in there myself, and that was only when I knew Every was out because I heard her heart hammering through the bedroom wall. That sound used to be the best thing in the world. Today it scares me.

I still have her letters, and I am crushed that I do. She's a mess, and either the letters aren't enough or she's not enough to see them. I don't know. I don't care. She's crying. Her arm is hurting, I suppose. Good. It should be. I hope her crying doesn't stop. Maybe in it she'll find what she would have failed to find in the letters. No way would she have appreciated them. I'll keep them. I don't know what I'll do with them. She's still here, though, and it's important.

She's still here.

Look, you're not, and I'm writing to you when I should be in there, with her, being her damn father. She's not at all what I wanted her to be, but neither am I. I have to do something about that. If I've failed her, I've failed you, and I know I've failed her. You left her with me after all and look what I did to your daughter. I ruined her. The fifth won't happen this year, Eleanor. It can't. And it won't again. Every and I have to be Every and I. That's all we have. So I don't know what to do with my letters to her, but my ones to you have to stop. Strangely, it's hard to stop writing. I know you're gone, and I know that writing has never kept you here, not really, but stopping is somehow hard. Habits are. I'm going to leave you with the only fifth you ever had - the one on which you died. You were in our bed, and then you were gone, and you have never returned. I said Goodbye then but I didn't mean it. I'm saying it now, meaning it (although I won't write it), so that I won't have to say it to our daughter. We can get there without you. We will have to. She's crying loudly as I say this: we'll miss you.

Love,
David

3/12/_____

Dear Dad,

I must have been wanting your letters while you were writing the last of them. Last night was so long you could have convinced me someone had stolen the sun. Eighteenth birthdays are supposed to be these cosmic events, these rites of passage, these times when your existence is celebrated by whatever group of people you have amassed in your time so far. Well, not me. I don't have one of those. I don't even have regret. I wish I could say I was lying, but when I think of what people my age are supposed to be like, and how they're meant to live, I doubt I'm missing out on much.

I sat on my alcove and I sat on my bed, and I pretended that listening out would let me hear your pen scratching the page. Silly, really. I thought you would be writing, and I wondered what it said. I thought you would write about the hospital, I thought you would write about your shame, I thought you would write about Mum. I thought maybe you would write down what you loved about me. Now that was a hole to fall into. Dear Every, it would say, these are the things I love: I love how you say Hello to me (once in a while), I love how you sleepwalk through school, I love how you hang your fringe sometimes so that I can't see your eyes, I love that I never have to see the friends you can only imagine, I love sitting in the hospital with you when you burn away at your liver, I love holding your hand when we're there and it feeling like assault, I love lying to you about your heart, I love messing with your heart, I love how I barely have to see you, I love how there are so many gashes in your arm that soon you'll have to use your leg, I love it when you're barely conscious, I love that you're better when you're barely conscious, I love when you're in pain, I laugh when you're in pain, I love that everything I dreamed of when you were born has gone to shit, I love that my life is shit, and I love you, you waste of skin - sure, I love you.

That's what I get for being awake through a long night. I can only appeal to your forgiveness and your sense of sympathy, as those thoughts battered my head for hours, and it was those hours that made me open up another pill bottle that I got from the doctor a while after the hospital trip. I took quite a few. I don't even know what they are, something -pram. I don't know how many I took but I slept hard as hell. In the morning my head was still full of it, all blocked up and skewed, and it was while the birds were beginning to sing outside that the burn in my stomach flared up. I couldn't bring myself to accept those letters. So I took another handful of pills and went downstairs to make breakfast. You know what happened after that.

My arm hurts, Dad, and I'm upset. The skin's going to peel quite badly. I'll probably help it along. But I want those letters. I do. I want to be the girl you wanted to give them to, the girl you used to look at and love, when the feelings could stop - no, stay - there.

I want to be Every. She sounds wonderful.

Love,
Eve

Dear Every,

I guess I have a couple more years. I've been reading these letters a lot lately, trying to decide whether or not they should end where they were supposed to. I still remember writing the first one. I remember it so well, actually, that sometimes I think I'm still writing it. One of the things I said in it (I have it here with me, let me get it right) was that if you were in the middle of hating me, then I could just give them to you on your twenty first birthday instead. I suppose I should be glad you don't hate me, at least not as far as I can see, but in a way that would have been an easier reason to wait. But I've decided, as you can tell, to keep writing these, and there will be no other option but to give them to you when you turn twenty one, because that's really my last chance. And it will be your last chance to have something to celebrate before all you can do is to start growing old.

I think you've accepted that your life, as it is, will pass. That's not to say it'll become something better, but it's something you've begun to wait out. I'm not sure how I feel about that. On the one hand it's good, because it means this isn't all you want, but I think you've resigned yourself to it as if it's made you too tired to help it on its way. I see that tiredness on your face. It's quite pretty. Innocent, truly, in the face of everything. I try to help, and you let me, because, I think, you want me to. You don't ever ask me to, though. That's something else you get from your dear old mother. Still, we managed on the fifth. We really did. I guess everything passes away if you let it.

We've spent some time together. More time. I let a lot of it go when you were younger, didn't I? We don't do much, just walk around in parks, and if it's warm outside then we sit and eat picnics. Feed the ducks. Those are pleasant afternoons. We look around at all the people neither of us know and we talk about what it would be like if we did know them. It would probably be nice, wouldn't it, that's what we both think. We walk around the water.

You cover your arm in public. Not so much at home. I guess that means you're learning something from the shame. You still hurt yourself, sometimes. And your walk is slow, because sometimes I think you're not as together as you are sure to make it seem. You do that for me, and I thank you, but you don't have to. Just be whatever you are, appear however you feel, and I'll stay with you until it goes. And if it doesn't go then I won't either.

I anger myself that I didn't offer that so much earlier. I wonder what that could have avoided. There's a lot about you that I wish never happened, and when we sit on picnic blankets I see a distance in your eyes and I know that I could have made it less severe if I hadn't learned about being a father so damn late. You're an adult, and it's only now that I feel ready to bring you up, and that is not fair on you, so I am sorry.

We don't go to the same parks I used to go to with your mother. I don't want to. I worry that I could fool myself in there. Sometimes I hear your heart coming out of your room, because you still think it's her, and I have moments when I trick myself into thinking that it is. Then I remind myself that it is you, and it gladdens me that it's still doing the same thing it was doing the day we made that recording. Sure, there are a few hiccups here and there, but it always catches back up.

That is not to say, though, that everything is fine. Everything is not. You don't keep it much of a secret that you still cut yourself, though I can see you're not doing it anywhere near as often as you used to. I guess that's a start. And when I look at you and your eyes are clouded and faraway, I kiss you on the forehead and stay with you until they return to the wonderful little hazel things I've been looking into all these years. Looking after you when you're like that doesn't make me mad anymore. I rather appreciate it that you let me.

Love,
Dad

3/12/_____

Dear Dad,

I'm glad you're still writing. I didn't know if you would. Only a couple more letters then? I suppose I only have a couple left to write myself. I expect I'll give mine to you some time, or maybe I'll write them out again into one big letter so you don't know I've been reading yours all this time. And I'm not sure how you'd feel about me reading the ones you wrote to Mum, so maybe it's better you don't know about that. I might just be writing to myself for now.

It has been three hundred and sixty four days since I gave myself this burn. I don't remember much about when it happened, but I remember there being pain, and I remember being on the floor. The rest - well, I took enough tablets that I hardly would have noticed if you'd hit me right in the face, or if Mum herself had walked in. It's strange how similar those two things seem now.

For a long time now, I have been so used to the scarred sight of my left arm that I barely notice it anymore. Even when I cut now, I just see a new wound against a pale patchwork of scars that a lot of the time are whiter than my skin. It's only if I can go a couple of weeks without doing it - and that does happen, every once in a while - that I'll catch myself looking at it closely, captivated, sometimes trying to trace them back to the first ones. It's impossible. I'll never see them again. My arm is so fucking corrugated. But I'm used to it.

The burn is an imposter. I think I took enough pills that I missed most of the shock when it happened, but it mapped itself onto my arm whether I knew about it or not. It softened very quickly, and in the flashes of near consciousness that I had while I sat on the floor, I saw a nearly perfect oval, softened and raised, overlapping a lot of my cuts, which looked as though they were reaching in with stickman bones. The colour didn't fade at the edges. There was no faint blending back to skin. It was like a stamp, all sudden and thick. By the time my head had cleared up, pus had pooled beneath the surface and the skin had begun to wrinkle. It was soft to the touch and sensitive as fuck. The pain was flaring, and even the lightest touch from a falling sleeve lit it up like it was happening all over again. The burn was so intense that just being awake bought tears to my eyes. It wasn't like cutting at all. Maybe we should have gone to the hospital, I don't know.

It hurt to lie in bed that night. I was used to wounds coming at will, but that one was vaguely accidental, and there was no way to sleep that could stop it burning. Each time the pain pulsated, my mind went back to the picture of me on the floor, slumped in shame, hearing you move around ever so little and staying the hell away from me. And each time it happened, the shame grew deeper and the footsteps moved differently, more ethereal, until the sound wouldn't leave my head at all. By morning I had gone back to the floor so many times and heard you move so much that I could no longer tell what the burn had actually been like, and how much of it I had driven, so amplified, through my mind and straight into where it could impersonate the memory. I wish I could say it was only like that for one night. I can't. I don't like burns.

We danced around in our famed avoidance of each other for what felt like weeks, and I suppose it may have been. I tried to acclimatise to the burn the way I imagine people have to get used to their jobs. The pain had worn off after a few days and I was left carrying around this bright red shape that I could only conceal by covering it up with clothes, and I'd got sick of doing that if I'm being honest about it. I started walking around the house in shorter sleeves, first by turning my arm in as far as I could. That was easy when it was just cuts because usually I only cut on the inside, but the burn was too big and spread out. And on one edge, where it laid over old scars, a collection of them shone through. Tally charts scratched into bark. That's the nearest thing I have to a photograph of myself. I wish people would just look at my arm instead of my face. That's where I am. There's nothing where my face is.

Well, that's a lie. You might remember the month, I forget exactly which it was, but it was one of the warmer ones. I know it was because I was hot enough to wear just a tank top, and that almost never happens. You were clearing up in the kitchen, and I walked in and watched you, and after a few seconds you stopped what you were doing, and you turned to me and smiled. God, that must have been such an effort. You held it there, painted onto you, and your chin began to quiver. You put down the tea towel and put your hands tightly inside one another.

I cried first. It was only a little, but I think it was the first time you had ever seen me cry. And it was the first time I had ever cried in front of someone willingly. I wiped some of the tears away and felt myself trying to contort my arm to hide it from you somehow, but after several flinches I gave up and dropped it, burns and scars be damned. I exhaled so hard it might have sounded like a sob. I wiped my eyes again. I wiped my whole face.

You did too.

It was around that time that we gave up hiding quite so much, from each other and from the world. We even left the house together, and it was you who convinced me to go out without covering my arm, just the once. We had been out for a fair few walks together by that point, and I guess you had noticed the ritual of me selecting either a jacket or a shawl, and staying out of the light let in by the open door until I was all covered up. We were heading out for a walk in the park one afternoon, a slow stroll around the pond where I had named the fish as a child. I felt the heat ripple inwards when you opened the door for us to leave, and I'll admit a little deflation when even the shawl seemed too burdensome for another day. Perhaps there was a little hesitation. Perhaps you saw it. As I peeled the shawl off the coathook you said, 'Why don't you leave that here?'

I hadn't stepped out of the house with bare arms since God knows when. The sun hadn't seen my arms in years. Walking around the park I felt like I was the only sepia object in a clear landscape but it turns out scars glisten in the sun.

Every few nights I slip. I find myself taking tablets and I don't know why. Who needs a reason. The thinking of it makes me do it too. It's like sometimes a day just has it in for me, and I end up dizzy with stomach pains. You check on me every night now, and I skirt consciousness enough to notice when you clean up my cuts. There's time in between them for each new cut to heal. I hope you've noticed that you don't need to clean me up now as much as you used to.

Love,
Eve x

Dear Every,

It is an unreserved revelation to me to have hosted dinner today with your friend Elsie. I had become so used to your persisting solitude that when you spoke of a friend, I was somehow surprised. There were some weeks between when you started to talk about her and when she came to eat with us, and those were weeks when I had to adjust to the idea that your life was no longer entwined only with mine. It was a grievance of sorts. A sprouting of jealousy. For however many years now, our lives have encompassed one other and resisted as well as they can the world's intrusion, but as much as part of me wanted desperately to keep you to myself, the thought that you had found someone that you were fond of enough to invite to our house hinted towards a potential, elusive comfort on your horizon that I honestly believed was beyond the reach of either of us. That used to apply to me when your mother was here, but comfort is a ghost now.

We had planned dinner for six o'clock. We like to eat early. Elsie was to arrive around five. Yesterday I made a small cake, and I must admit to watching an ungodly number of sitcoms on TV to see how people get ready for a dinner - our table is nowhere near the size it would need to be to pull off some of the things I saw. So I had to make it up. Before today, the nearest I have been to a real dinner in a decade is the odd time you and I have sat at the same table through happenstance and convenience. It's just not something we've done. I used to make some of the food when you were small, but honestly, why lie, your mother took care of most of it.

I set the table the way I'd seen it on TV. I laid the fancy plates out ahead of time with the cutlery to the side, and a water jug was just off centre, leaving space for a big wooden board for the dinner to go on when it came out of the oven. I got the third chair out of the shed. We hadn't needed it in a long, long time.

And I bought flowers. A lot of people like flowers.

You came downstairs a little while before Elsie arrived, and you had done your version of dressing up for the occasion. Your hair was down, and neat, and there was the faintest makeup around your eyes. You had your shawl on.

'Hey,' you said. 'This is nice.'

You touched the back of a chair lightly, and you looked over the table, and you appeared, for once, not to carry too much thought with you. The lines around your eyes eased out into your momentarily smooth face. And there my mind went, forcing on me an attempt to create its own photographs from what it saw. 'There's chicken,' I said. 'Roasted.' I thought words might break the thought.

'Ooh, chicken.'

'Do you want to see your cake?'

'No. After.'

'Okay.'

I went to get the wine from the cupboard. I honestly didn't know if that was a great idea. I didn't know if that was too much temptation for you, but everything I'd seen on those crappy comedies seemed to say that dinners had wine with them. I got red.

You were sat at the table when I got back, tucked away in the corner of the room so that you'd need to ask either me or Elsie to move if you needed the toilet. That's a funny place to pick when you've got the choice, but I guess you like it in the corner. I poured us half a glass each, and I sat with you. You sipped at it. We'd cope if you just sipped at it. When you spoke to me the smell was very strong.

'I'm hungry,' you said.

'Well, good timing I suppose.' I meant to say it with a laugh. 'Every,' I said, 'I'm sorry we haven't done this before.'

'Don't worry.'

'But I am. We should have done this more. I'm sorry we haven't.'

'Yeah, okay.'

'Shit,' I said, probably too quickly, and probably too loudly. You sat back, and for a moment your chin dropped and you looked almost frightened. I had not meant to shout, if that is what I did. I'm sorry for that, too. You know what, I'm getting tired of being sorry. I really am.

'What's wrong?'

The candles. 'I forgot the candles.' I jumped up and started rummaging around for where I'd put them.

'It's okay. Don't worry.'

'No, we should have candles. Dinners have candles.' I found them at the front of the cupboard. I must have looked past them ten times already. I set them down beside the jug. The candleholders were old and a little dusty, two of those old silver looking things, all curls and shine. I lit a match, and then I paused. The flame burned towards me. 'I should have asked. Do you want candles?'

You looked at the match, and you looked at me. Then you nodded, somewhat involuntarily it seemed. 'I like candles.' I went ahead and lit them.

There was silence or nearly silence for half an hour or so. I didn't mind it. We've come a long way, us two, but it doesn't exactly make us a pair of chatterboxes. Still, the quiet wasn't one to endure, nor was it filled with the regret of what should have been said. It was tolerable. I hope my company is tolerable.

You answered the door just as I was finishing up dinner. You muttered some words quietly and Elsie stepped inside, and I turned to see all the way down the hall. You were silhouettes from there. The occasional flicker of light caught the rim of Elsie's glasses. Other children welcomed friends when they were four or five. Other parents hosted when their children were still children. We are late bloomers. I waited for you to bring Elsie through. She didn't look too dissimilar to you - a little taller perhaps, and a steeper brow, but beyond that and some darker hair, an artist would use the same shapes. 'Dad, this is Elsie.'

'Hi,' she said.

'Hello.' I was a little surprised it was Hello that came out and not Hi. I thought Hi sounded friendlier, more worn in through the years. And I found myself sticking out a hand, which Elsie politely shook. 'Please do sit down,' I said.

'Thanks.'

I turned to get some crackers, and I felt my movements grow heavier, as though my veins were painted onto rock. I took a deep breath and turned back to you. You were both sitting, and talking quietly enough that it appeared my presence wasn't needed there. You had removed your shawl, which was hanging from the back of the chair. Your arm was on the table, centre stage. You weren't hiding at all. There was someone you weren't hiding at all from.

I sat with you.

We ate.

I hope I will see your friend again.

Love,
Dad

3/12/_____

Dear Dad,

Thank you. Dinner was lovely. Elsie said she liked you and she'd come to eat again. Look at us socialites! I will admit to some tears after we finished eating, when Elsie was leaving, when you insisted I let you wash up after us. I went upstairs and sat in the alcove. I played the sound of my heart, beating arrhythmically over the patter in my chest. The house was quiet, and you are right, it was bearable, and I let the tears fall there, and they were happy ones, or at least ones of relief. You used to worry that everything about me came from Mum, but now you know there's something that only ever really came from you. Thank you.

I met Elsie at college. There's a bench I always eat at, and there was a very hot day when the sun hung above us, and it seemed like everyone in the building wanted to eat under it. Elsie walked over to the bench and placed her shadow over me. I didn't look up right away.

'Do you have a lighter?' she asked.

'No.'

She didn't go away. I sat there, the way you freeze when you need someone to leave, and I stared into her shadow. A glow fought at the edges.

'Is anyone sitting here?'

'No.'

She still didn't go.

'Can I sit here?'

'Yes.' You're supposed to say Yes.

Elsie sat down and pulled her shadow away from me. I toyed with the rest of my sandwich, but it was just so damn hot that day. I don't know why I was outside at all - I don't even like the heat. Elsie sat over the bench from me and started on her lunch. I kept my eyes on my sandwich crumbs. It wasn't long before the feeling that she was staring at me elevated itself to knowing. I had rolled my sleeves up because of the heat, and I'd forgotten to roll them down when Elsie sat with me. Scars really can itch in the sun.

'Hey,' she said. I hesitated, but it seemed impolite not to look. My left eye twitched a little. She rolled her own sleeve back and put her arm on the bench. She had even more cuts than me, and some of them were a heck of a lot more recent. One was closed, but only just. Hers were a lot deeper than mine and the scars were like hills. They kind of put mine to shame. I know I shouldn't think about it like that, but well, I do. I rolled my sleeve down and Elsie put her arm away. 'I'm Elsie,' she said.

'Eve. I'm Eve.'

And that was it. Who needs conversation.

We had a few lunches together, and we sat together in the classes we shared. Elsie would stitch under the table when she was bored, which meant Elsie stitched a lot. She's good. She taught me that stitching keeps your head busy, and I guess she's right, so I try to do that every now and again. All I've ever managed is a couple of handkerchiefs, with a pale blue stripe down the side of one of them, but I like them enough. I suppose it only matters that I like them.

I am looking forward to having Elsie over again. I am looking forward to having a friend here. And I wonder what I may have missed out on, while we wore our broken thoughts like boots. Well, I guess I won't know. That's a waste of a thought. Then again, most of them have been.

I guess these might be tears of regret. They might be tears of hope. Maybe those aren't different. This time next year, we can share our letters, and I will take my time reading them as the need to hide them will have gone. I will say Thank You when you give them to me, I'll say Thank You now, and I don't know what I'll say to you after that, but I suppose I have a while to think. I hope you like mine. Maybe one day we can thread them together like lace.

I started this letter saying that my happy tears were the thing that came from you and not Mum. They are drying up, and I'll remember them fondly, but since they started I've realised something else: I write like you, Dad.

Love,
Eve

Dear Eleanor,

Every has been gone for days. I have not seen much of her recently, a little less each day as the days themselves wore on, and I cannot pinpoint exactly when it was that she left. If you had asked me an hour ago I'd have said the last time I saw her was four or five days ago when she came home from an evening walk and hung her coat up on the hook, but since then I have remembered her making me tea the next morning. And after that, I have a fleeting image in my mind of the TV being on as I walked past the living room, and a little later on it was off. I didn't switch it off, so she can't have been gone then. I wonder how many more momentary memories will squeeze themselves into that time between then and now, when I am sure she is gone.

Her heartbeat has played constantly for weeks, and a few days ago even I grew tired of it being as loud as it was, so I knocked on her door to ask her to turn it down. It comforts her though, it really does. She didn't answer, so I opened the door, and she wasn't inside. I said her name, and I repeated it louder so that she could hear it over the heartbeat. No response - no child. The bedsheets were tidy. The curtains were drawn and tied back neatly. The sun poured in and the echo of the heartbeat thudded into the floor. Her wardrobe and drawers were not quite empty, but her favourite clothes were gone. Her shawl was missing from the hook on her door. And on top of the wardrobe, dust clung on around the empty space where her backpack used to be.

I turned the heartbeat down. My hand hovered around the switch but I couldn't bring myself to turn it off. It was faint.

At first, I stayed awake at night, and I stayed put. The days changed around clothes that did not. This brown and yellow check shirt probably can't take too many more washes. I have had the same stone cold teacup in my hand for hours at a time. It is Every that makes the tea, usually. The will to move more than my eyes receded like a tide, and I could see the door from my chair in the kitchen. The postman would arrive at around the same time each day, and I would tell myself in the run up to it that he was coming, that it wasn't Every, and that his shape through the window was going to do all it could to fool me. And fool me it did, every time. I have never lived with much hope, but I know desperation. A pain flared in the front of my head, right over my eyes, from the refusal to sleep for even a minute, and eventually I jumped up, in a dying down afternoon, in an attempt to stave off sleep. Movements had never felt more like creaks, and breathing no more like a slur.

I left the house that evening for the first time in days. In a way it felt more like a betrayal leaving an empty house than to leave it when she was home, in case, I guess, she'd come back while I was gone. I opened the door and the air rushed at me. It knocked me back a little. I walked those streets like a god damn hound. I turned to check every doorway and the faces that emerged from them. From far away the backs of heads looked like dots, and they were so small, and I scanned them all so fast, and I widened my eyes to them as they turned and came closer, displaying momentary expressions on countenances I had not known. I didn't know any of them. I never had. Part of me wished I had known just a few. Just for a time. Well I guess I knew Christopher, and what was her name, Mia.

The dusk seemed to persist a little longer than it usually does this time of year, and as far as I'm concerned it did it for me. The streets started emptying of people the nearer to dark it got. None of them were Every. The streetlights offered pale platitudes just in front them, but short of standing under one and probably freaking the shit out of everyone who passed by, they were useless.

I went a little further and found myself a couple of streets away from Elsie's house. I went there. The front of the house had a couple of bushes rising above the wall so that you couldn't see the living room windows. The path was paved and part of it was cracking. I rang the doorbell. It was Elsie's dad who answered. Maybe he was her stepdad, I'm not sure. Either way, I hadn't met him before. He was around the same age as me but a good deal taller. I looked up with my eyes and then with my neck.

'Yes?' he said.

'Oh.' I hesitated. Someone my age asking for someone Elsie's age was never going to look good. 'I'm sorry to disturb you. Is Elsie here?'

'Who are you, if you don't mind me asking?'

'I'm her friend's dad. My daughter is Every.'

He shook his head slightly.

'Eve?' I asked.

'No, sorry. What do you want with Elsie?'

'I... my daughter is missing. I thought Elsie might have seen her.'

'Goodness,' the man said, nodding in stuttering bursts. He called for Elsie. She came to the foot of the stairs and her dad gave way to her. He stood behind her. 'Do you know this man?' he asked.

'Yeah,' she said. She was picking loose cotton out of her top. I noticed that her arms were covered up.

'Have you seen Every?' I asked.

'No. Why?'

'She's missing.'

'Oh God.' Her arms dropped. 'Since when?'

'I don't know. A day. A couple of days maybe. I think it's been a few nights.'

Elsie looked at me like the words were out of order. And who knows, maybe they were. 'Have you seen her?'

'No, I haven't.'

'Please.'

'I haven't seen her.'

'Have you - when did you last see her?'

'I, um... I haven't spoken to her in weeks.'

'What do you mean?'

'I haven't seen her. I kept trying to call her but she stopped answering. That's it really. I'm sorry.'

'I don't get it,' I said. 'I thought you two were close.'

'We were. We're not now. I'm sorry.'

'Well, what happened? Was she upset?'

'Nothing happened.'

I let out some air loudly. I guess I was holding onto it too hard.

Elsie's dad stepped forward and asked, 'Have you spoken to the police?'

'No. Not yet.'

'Well, I think you should.'

'Do you want help finding her?' Elsie asked.

'No,' I said. 'That's okay. But thank you.'

I turned and shambled off. I heard them murmuring behind me, probably about me, until their door closed and blocked their voices out. As I walked every street and alley I could find, I found myself wishing that Every had some kind of favourite place I could go to, somewhere where I knew she, at the very least, *might* be. She had never really painted herself into the town. She had only ever been to places where the obligation persisted. The school. The supermarket when we were low on milk. I remembered all those times she had come home like clockwork on the fifth, and even more all those times she had never left the house to begin with. It's not like I hadn't gone days without seeing her before, but before at least I knew she was in her room. Then again, maybe she wasn't. Maybe this is what she does, maybe it's something else about her I've failed to know. I don't think so. If this had happened when she was fifteen I think I could believe it was some kind of mood, some temporary absence that she would return from, but she has been too much a part of my daily life in the last couple of years that I just don't believe it. She has come too far. You would be proud - she may have come further than you did. I cannot tell if the insistent recollections I have right now of her eating breakfast with me, walking with me, not hiding her skin from me - Jesus, even talking to me - I cannot tell if they are memories or taunts, but I am certain that they are easier to dwell on than the bleeding and absence I've lived with so much before now.

It was at around two in the morning, after I had not just not seen her, but had not seen anyone for hours, that I found myself sticking the key in the lock and stepping back into the house. I promise that I was not closing the door on the chance that she was out there, but I did not know where else to go. That night I at least went to bed, and although all I did was sit in it with the covers around my ankles and the lamps casting yellow around me, I suppose it was better than the chair. I have a lot of time left to sit in the chair, and to wait.

The evenings since have been no different. Neither have the nights or the dawns. I must fall asleep here and there but it doesn't last. I don't want it to. If she steps foot back in the house, I want to know when her sole touches the carpet.

Midnight passed an hour ago and I have been writing for three. I have all these letters to give to her and she is not here to read them. I've flicked through them all so many times now that I know them by heart. Well, of course I do. They started there after all. There was one year, the year after you left, that I actually wrote two letters with the thought that one day I would decide which one to give her. One was about when you died. The other was about when we met. I thought I had decided - the one about the folk festival has been in the envelope for months now. But I kept the other one too, and it is now back in the envelope where it was. And I'm going to leave it there, because at the end of the day - at the end of every day - both of those things happened.

And so I find myself, again, writing to a memory. I, a clean shaven twenty something, used to write to a future I thought I could reach. Now, I feel like a fool. I used to write Every letters when you and her were near to me, imagining at once what to say to her, and what my life would be like when she read it. I watched terribly closely as life happened to you, and took you, and I have only ever really watched Every from the sidelines. I remember working in the garden one summer when we'd barely had any rain, and Every watched me from the path - to this day I don't think she's so much as watered the tomatoes out there. She was behind me, and I heard her move, and I heard the rake scrape the floor. There was a thick thudding sound. Every winced. I turned my head only a little, almost involuntarily, and saw the outline of her foot over the head of the rake. She stepped on it again and there was a blur, a thud, and a curse within the wince. I turned back to the plants. 'Hey, look how hard it goes,' she said. Her voice sounded like it was coming from a tin can. 'It goes right up under my chin.'

'I'm not looking,' I said.

'Look.'

She did it again.

'I'm not looking.'

I heard a couple more thuds, then heavy breathing in place of more.

'I'll put this away,' she said.

I hope that's what she's done.

Love,
David

Printed in Great Britain
by Amazon